All That Matters

This Large Print Book carries the Seal of Approval of N.A.V.H.

All That Matters

Jan Goldstein

Thorndike Press • Waterville, Maine

Published in 2004 by arrangement with Hyperion, an imprint of Buena Vista Books, Inc.

Thorndike Press® Large Print Basic.

The tree indicium is a trademark of Thorndike Press.

The text of this Large Print edition is unabridged.
Other aspects of the book may vary from the original edition.

Set in 16 pt. Plantin by Christina S. Huff.

Printed in the United States on permanent paper.

Library of Congress Cataloging-in-Publication Data

Goldstein, Jan.
    All that matters / Jan Goldstein.
        p. cm.
    ISBN 0-7862-6951-0 (lg. print : hc : alk. paper)
    1. Young women — Fiction.   2. Grandmothers —
Fiction.   3. Despair — Fiction.   4. Large type books.
I. Title.
PS3607.O4844A78 2004b
813´.6—dc22   2004056695

For my mother,
whom my children knew as Nana.
More than anyone,
it was she who taught me how to recognize
all that matters.

As the Founder/CEO of NAVH, the only national health agency solely devoted to those who, although not totally blind, have an eye disease which could lead to serious visual impairment, I am pleased to recognize Thorndike Press* as one of the leading publishers in the large print field.

Founded in 1954 in San Francisco to prepare large print textbooks for partially seeing children, NAVH became the pioneer and standard setting agency in the preparation of large type.

Today, those publishers who meet our standards carry the prestigious "Seal of Approval" indicating high quality large print. We are delighted that Thorndike Press is one of the publishers whose titles meet these standards. We are also pleased to recognize the significant contribution Thorndike Press is making in this important and growing field.

Lorraine H. Marchi, L.H.D.
Founder/CEO
NAVH

* Thorndike Press encompasses the following imprints: Thorndike, Wheeler, Walker and Large Print Press.

Acknowledgments

All That Matters would never have been possible without the nurturing and remarkable dedication of my amazing agent, Linda Chester. Her belief in me has put wings on my dreams. I'm so grateful to her executive manager, Gary Jaffe, whose gracious assistance with all things large and small makes my world a better place.

I am thankful beyond measure for Kyra Ryan's brilliant reading and suggestions with the manuscript. Her discerning eye and caring heart were integral as this novel found its footing.

Let me say at the start that Hyperion is quite simply the class of publishing. Gretchen Young, my editor, fell in love with this novel the moment she read it and told me we each need a grandmother like Gabby in our lives. Her hard work and vision have touched me with grace. Bob Miller, the president of Hyperion, is truly a prince in the publishing business. All writers should be so lucky. And Ellen Archer, my publisher, has taken this book under her wing and personally shepherded its journey. I am deeply indebted. I send my thanks out to others in the wondrous Hyperion family: Jane Comins and her hardworking marketing staff; Natalie Kaire in editorial; Karin Maake, a dream of a publicist; Hyperion's art department, which designed the touchingly beautiful cover; Zareen Jaffery, for tireless assistance in meeting editorial deadlines; and to the rest of the incredible staff: the production people, the book reps — all who have been instrumental in bringing *All That Matters* into readers' hands.

To Pearl Brown and Jack Berman, dear friends, who provided me a mountain retreat where much of this book was written — my appreciation knows no bounds.

Thanks to all of my friends for their inspiration and good humor, and special appreciation to Lili and Jon Bosse, Russ and Rebecca Landau, and to Richard Carlson for their heartfelt efforts in support of this book.

My gratitude to my in-laws, Matt and Marion Solomon, who provide not only ongoing encouragement but bike rides and brunches that prove essential to clearing the mind.

To my children, Yaffa, Batsheva, Elisha,

Ari, and Shira, and, by extension, their significant others — Chris, Andy, and Stefanie (and further extensions Asher, Shai, Isabella, and Chaz): You teach me to reach beyond the stars. Thanks for all your love, for all the hugs and all the hope.

And finally, to Bonnie, my beautiful wife, cheerleader extraordinaire, and best friend — your love and exuberant support matter beyond measure!

Author's Note

When I was a young boy my father's first cousin, Fania Ingber, shared with me the story of how she survived the Nazis: hiding in the forest as a young girl and later in the attic of a righteous woman for two years. Those details help inform the character of Gabby. Through her I humbly pay tribute to all the survivors, the Fanias of the world, each with his or her own indomitable spirit.

1

It had all gone wrong, of course.

No one was supposed to notice her there in the sand on the Venice, California, beach at sunset. Why would they? A human circus of all shapes, hair colors, and states of mind gathered along the shore to witness the orgasmic reds and resplendent golds at the end of each day. A five-foot-three mousy-haired, slightly built young woman in this crowd was like a rerun in the middle of television's new fall lineup — who's going to bother tuning in? It was a perfect plan.

Thing was, Jennifer had reasoned with a cynic's clarity, anybody could end her life behind closed doors. But why wade through the morass of possible distractions that her indoor suicide might occasion? Prolonging the inevitable with one more late-night movie on the tube. Stumbling on yet another marathon chat session among similarly depressed individuals on the Internet. The temptation to humiliate herself with pitiful phone calls to the living heartache who'd once masqueraded as her soul mate.

Everything up to that point —

the brisk twenty-minute walk to the beach;
the glorious farewell sunset;
the tying to her waist of her ever-present camcorder with the simple 411 that, in the cool, dispassionate adding-up of her life, the minuses simply outnumbered the pluses;
the slightly hyperventilating intake of drugs and alcohol, allowing her to drift off on a cloud of Xanax and tequila —

all of it had gone just as Jennifer had envisioned.

But then the one thing that was not supposed to happen actually did. Some time after she had laid her head down and passed out, the truck hauling the large metal comb used for grooming the sand nearly ran over the inert object in its path and, just like that . . . someone noticed.

Afterward, a flurry of doctors, nurses, and medical assistants floated around Jennifer's bed. Hours passed in which she was in and out of consciousness. At one point she looked up through the haze of her stupor to see her father's face bobbing overhead. *How does he do it* — the question poked through her fog — *even now, not a hair out of place?* She hadn't known he could cry. *Where were you when I could have used some of this attention?* her brain shouted. She wished he would go back to his little wife and his baby, leave her the hell alone. He used to do that so well.

And then he *was* gone, leaving her with her failure.

Later, amid the lights, the voices, and the churning within her, Jennifer fell into a fitful sleep and dreamed of her mother. In the dream, Lili stood on a massive rock overlooking a body of water. From this stone formation she appeared to be throwing something out into the sea. But Jennifer couldn't recall having ever been to this place she saw now in her dream. Why was her mother on this strange rock? And what was she discarding?

When Jennifer awoke the next morning she was still groggy and confused. But confusion was about to meet its match.

2

Jennifer stared at a worn and wrinkled face. The flesh was age-spotted, mere wisps of hair stood in for eyebrows, and the head was crowned with a floating halo of white hair, looking as ethereal and comic as Einstein's. Nevertheless, the blue eyes twinkled with life and the face was as animated as a child's. Jennifer felt a brief tug of emotion, an ache to reach out to the safe haven of arms that had once soothed the wounds of a broken home. But these feelings quickly disappeared and Jennifer recoiled, shrinking back from the figure before her. She was facing the only person on earth who she knew truly cared about her. That made her grandmother the last person Jennifer wanted to see.

"Why are you here?" she demanded.

"My granddaughter is in a hospital. Where else should I be?" the old woman replied, reaching out to cup her granddaughter's wan face in a delicate, vein-laced hand.

"No, you're not supposed to," said Jennifer, pulling back like a cornered animal looking for a way out.

The older woman hushed her with the nod of a head and the twinkle of her hope-filled eyes. But the optimism slowly drained out of her face, as if Jennifer's gaze had pricked a hole in it, as the two stared at each other. Jennifer could read the pain in her nana's face and hated her for it, for being there in her room, for laying eyes upon her. She stared dispassionately now at the tired old woman. She noticed her nana's eyelids were crusted over and her cheeks were covered with a clownlike goop that tried to pass itself off as rouge. No, this wasn't the nana she remembered. A corrosion had taken place in the five years since Lili's funeral. Maybe this is why Nana had stayed away, Jennifer thought to herself, to keep me from witnessing the disintegration of someone who meant so much to me. That and the fact that — the horrible thought flashed in her mind — my nana should have died, not my mother.

"You really shouldn't be here, Nana. Who told you, anyway?" Jennifer complained, shaking her head with contempt.

The old woman shook her head. She was certain this was the depression talking, a sickness that had taken root in her grand-daughter's soul.

"Your father may not be the world's finest human being," she replied with a knowing smile that reflected she knew all too well the truth of her remark, "but he still knows enough to inform the people who matter. He's out there in the hallway now. He tells me he's married, Cynthia, I think her name is, with a baby, no less. I had no idea. But then, who would there be to tell me such things?" Nana chided gently.

"Look, I don't need the guilt, all right? I'm not the goddamn news service for my father's reinvented life. What's he doing out there anyway?" Jennifer pursed her lips in defiance and stared at the door.

"I'm sure he's worried about you. We are all worried about you," Nana whispered softly.

The only thing he's worried about is how much this will set him back, Jennifer told herself. That and whether or not the publicity will affect his next film project. Having a daughter try to take her life might scare off investors. Jennifer shook her head, mind racing at the possibilities. Then again, the man is an opportunist. He's Harvey Weinstein in a size 40. He'll no doubt play this for PR he couldn't buy in this town.

"He's probably out there right now giving an interview. The concerned parent pulling at the heartstrings of every reporter he can corner," Jennifer blurted out. "Barry Stempler in his glory!"

Her grandmother turned her head away, stunned by the pain and despair in the young woman. Jennifer was like a stranger to her. And yet, in spite of her granddaughter's grimace and the hurtful words, Nana glimpsed her daughter's face there. She was reminded of the sweet-faced girl Jennifer once was, one who, on a visit to New York City years back, had surprised everyone by clambering atop a display case at Macy's and launching into a spectacular tap dance. That little dancer had a grin that filled her pixie face and her eyes had lit up brighter than the ball dropped on New Year's Eve.

Gabby reached out to stroke her forehead and Jennifer closed her eyes tightly, as if the touch of her nana's loving hand brought more pain than she could bear.

"You know, meydele," Nana said softly, "I came all this way and flew on that plane where they shoehorn you into a seat meant for a small dog, not a person, just so I could tell you something . . . that I love you. Do you hear me?"

Jennifer clenched her fists and turned her

face away. Nana eased herself onto the far end of the bed as her granddaughter remained cocooned in her silence. The elderly woman exhaled sharply and, with a raspy groan, drew in a labored breath. Then, holding her frail hands together as if in prayer, Gabby whispered, "I came so you should know, and this I want you to remember even in this bad place in which you find yourself right now — you are not alone, Jennifer. You are never alone."

Gittel "Gabby" Zuckerman was the kind of woman you wanted in your corner when the chips were down — in fact, *especially* if they were down. From her outward appearance, of course, you would never guess this in a million years. Short, her once robust frame shrunken with age, she walked slightly hunched over, both from sheer mileage and the physical strain of drawing breath. She had moxie and a thirst for living that at times annoyed her more sedentary peer group. Her husband, Itzik, dead these past twenty-one years, used to say Gabby could outsmart half of New York and outrun the other. And yet there was a softness about her, especially when it came to family.

At seventy-six she still managed to get around. The effort, however, was now hampered by serious damage to her lungs, the result of a lifelong vice — smoking. While he was living, Itzik had urged her to give up the habit long before not smoking was fashionable. But Gabby had remained characteristically stubborn — in this case, to a fault. In the last year, she'd had to bow to the inevitable as the hacking, the wheezing, and the bouts of breathlessness, all courtesy of her emphysema, forced her to agree belatedly that the condition was killing her. Though the damage had already been done, she resolutely refused to give in to the verdict. Gabby preferred to see her condition as an opportunity to test herself, a challenge to be met. She might have to slow down some, but she would not be stopped.

And it was this indomitable inner core one might never suspect passing her on the sidewalks of the West Side of Manhattan, an area she had called home for thirty-seven years. Inside this ruddy, wrinkled skin beat the heart of one of life's true survivors.

Gabby's heart ached for Jennifer, who had become a bundle of rage. It was a grandmother's pain, one that reached the deepest part of her, a place where the memory of lost family resided. She yearned to share with Jennifer the tale of her own pain, of how she had once begged for her life to end. But her granddaughter was not ready to hear the story. Gabby conjured up the face of her younger sister, Anna, who had been robbed of the opportunity to reach her later teen years, much less her twenties. And here was Jennifer at twenty-three, balled up in her bed, her knees drawn up in a fetal position. A sudden anger spiked in Gabby. Why should her granddaughter so callously dismiss life?

But the sight of the troubled girl melted Gabby's resentment. Her eyes took in her granddaughter's pale arm where the IV needle fed life-giving fluids. Gabby's forehead creased with worry and beads of sweat formed in the furrows of her brow. And there in that hospital room she swore on Lili's memory that she would help Jennifer find her way out of the darkness and back into the light.

3

The supervising nurse on the ward reported to Barry Stempler that what his daughter needed now more than ever was love and support. There must be no confrontations, absolutely nothing that might provoke her. This warning Barry had taken to heart by showing up in Jennifer's room the following morning with his second wife, Cynthia, and their baby girl in tow. Gabby, who had arrived minutes earlier from the motel down the block, exchanged perfunctory niceties with her ex-son-in-law and Ms. Beverly Hills Aerobics. Instinctively she reached out to pinch the cheek of the chubby infant clinging to Barry. But Gabby's eye caught her granddaughter's and saw a flicker of betrayal. She pulled her hand away from the baby, quickly moving to the side of the room.

Jennifer observed her father. He was, as always, incapable of standing still, a human windmill: hands gesticulating, bouncing on his heels, zigzagging the room, eyes moving from face to face to make sure he had everyone's attention. Here he was now, playing with his new daughter, hoisting her onto his shoulders, then twirling her back into his arms as the infant cooed happily. The kid reminded Jennifer of a Chihuahua. All the while, Barry's attention bounced back and forth from his baby to Jennifer, as if to say, "Hey, Jen, check it out. You don't have to kill yourself to get my attention. I'm here for you, see? I can do this." *You narcissistic bastard,* she thought, turning away.

Off to one side, Ms. Beverly Hills Aerobics was blathering about some exciting new fitness program that would soon have Jennifer "back in the swing of things" where she belonged. There was only one problem — Jennifer didn't *want* to get back in the swing of things. In fact, the only thing she felt like doing was getting that annoyingly cute baby out of her face.

After twenty minutes, this farce was interrupted by the buzz of Barry's beeper. He examined the message in the tiny window as if it were life and death. "Bastards," he muttered, glancing up and catching Gabby's look of disapproval. "If I'm not on the set supervising, then you can be sure everything goes straight to hell," he offered in his own defense. "Nice of you to fly all this way,

Gabby. I'm sure Jen appreciates that. Right, Jen?" Jennifer stared out the window. "Look, I gotta run, but I'll catch you later. That's a promise." Gabby thought Barry looked relieved as he waved good-bye and quickly ushered his new family out the door.

With Barry, the wife, and the Chihuahua gone, the room suddenly felt very still. It was as if a tornado had swept through and left nothing but silent wreckage in its wake. Gabby watched as Jennifer closed her eyes and leaned back against the pillow, releasing air from deep within her. *Is it possible,* Gabby thought, *that Jennifer has been holding her breath the entire time her father was in the room?* Gabby noticed how the muscles in Jennifer's neck and jaw loosened, as if a belt cinched too tightly around a waist was now being let out.

Gabby looked on curiously as Jennifer eyed a small case sitting on a side table next to her bed. It rested there alongside a pitcher of water, plastic glasses, and a well-thumbed copy of the latest *People*. Jennifer seemed to have just discovered it, though Gabby had seen it there when she arrived a day earlier.

Jennifer leaned over and grabbed the case. Reaching in it, she pulled out the camcorder. She remembered how she had tied it to herself on the beach. She opened the cartridge window and checked for the tape. It was still in there. Jennifer wondered if the doctors or her dad had seen it. And if so, why had they given it back to her?

"A gift?" her grandmother inquired, startling Jennifer. Gabby had been so uncharacteristically quiet Jennifer had forgotten she was in the room.

"It's mine," Jennifer answered curtly.

"Is this a career choice or a hobby?" Gabby ventured, looking for a way into any conversation.

But Jennifer ignored her. As Gabby observed from across the room, Jennifer idly panned without recording the bare walls, the sterile plastic IV bottles lying on a nearby counter, the bedpan atop a chair by the wall. When the camera found Gabby, leaning awkwardly against the windowsill, Gabby attempted to catch her granddaughter's eye through the glass lens, trying to comprehend where and who Jennifer was. Jennifer relentlessly pressed the zoom button, snapping Gabby's image into a warped, disfiguring close-up and then pushing her away with a jarring zoom out. Through all this, Gabby's gaze did not falter, even though the open eye of the lens staring unblinkingly at her was causing her discomfort.

What was it Jennifer saw through this machine? Gabby wondered. And what, if anything, did she hope to see?

4

The next day Gabby stood alongside Barry and his wife in the hospital office of Dr. Waldo Green as the rumpled middle-aged supervisor of psychiatric services made his recommendation.

"Often we'll see remorse immediately after a failed attempt. Jennifer hasn't really displayed any. To be frank, she hasn't opened up much to any of us. She's angry, and that feeds her depression. On the plus side, her anger is a sign of life. She hasn't chosen to turn it off. That's a good thing. In addition, the staff and I have noted that her rare outbursts show she possesses a sharp intellect, even a flash of wit."

"That's my daughter. Nothing wrong in the brains department," Barry blurted out. Gabby shot him a look of disapproval.

"Normally we have a seventy-two-hour hold. In cases like this," Green continued, "until we get some positive indication from the patient, it's our recommendation to hold on to the individual."

"So that's the plan, to hold her in the psych ward?" Barry jumped in, nodding his agreement. "Because I want her to get the best care, but clearly she doesn't belong on the streets. I mean, she needs help that none of us can give her."

Green took off his glasses and massaged his eyes. Gabby studied him carefully.

"Your daughter took a fair amount of Xanax," Green noted, reviewing his files. "I'd like to see some regret, feel that she's not going to try it again, yes. But this is a first attempt, so I must tell you we're not going to hold her for long."

"Wait a minute. You'd let her out of here?" Barry shifted, hands waving, voice rising in anger. "But you said . . ."

"Well, she is over twenty-one. Of course I do have some discretion in this matter. If she continues showing signs of contempt, I'd have to keep her under supervision and you would have to cover costs." He paused, adding offhandedly, "Then again, if she's willing to make a contract with me, I could always release her into your care."

Gabby observed as Barry and Cynthia exchanged a look of quiet panic.

"That might not be such a . . . what I mean is . . ." Barry offered haltingly before his wife jumped in.

"With a baby it doesn't seem like a very good idea to have someone in Jennifer's condition around," Cynthia stammered defensively. "And then there's the new film Barry's working on. You have no idea the demands on his time."

"There must be other places she can go," Barry insisted, "you know, to get well. I'll take care of the money end, no problem," he asserted with bravado, his wife nodding eagerly beside him. "I want you to put her in the *best damn institution* you have!"

Green nodded, catching a sneeze in his wrinkled handkerchief. "We could do that." He shrugged.

No one had noticed Gabby shaking her head as vigorously as if she were objecting to a death sentence. And now she was ready to burst.

"I did not hide away in an attic, jump from Hitler's death train, and escape the burning hell of Poland to see my granddaughter locked up in some loony bin," she announced suddenly, startling the other three. "Jennifer is not crazy, she's lost. She's going home with me!"

Stunned, Barry exploded with a ferocity usually reserved for directors who'd gone over-budget. "Are you out of your mind?" he screamed, advancing on her. "Look,

Gabby, I gave you a call because it was the right thing to do. You're her grandmother, know what I mean? But I think I know what's in my daughter's best interests!"

"Barry," Gabby replied, pulling herself up to her full five foot one and change, "you wouldn't know her best interests if they walked up and bit you in the tokhes."

"Hmmm," interjected the squat physician, smoothing wisps of hair across his balding pate, his eyes coming to life for the first time at Gabby's declaration. "Actually, Mr. Stempler, it might not be such a terrible idea to have Jennifer spend a little time with family. That is one approach we've used. One view is that it can prove more successful for postsuicidal treatment than keeping the patient locked up. Quite frankly," he continued, raising his eyebrows a notch as he glanced at Barry and the wife, "given the circumstances I hadn't thought that was a possibility."

Barry's eyes flashed in defiance. He pulled the doctor aside.

"You don't know this woman, Doctor," he said in agitation. "She's been out of the picture. Lives in New York. This would be nuts."

"I'm just saying that having her with someone she loves, even if she herself can't *feel* love right at the moment, could prove beneficial. In this case, Jennifer might respond to having contact with a nonthreatening member of her family."

"What the hell is that supposed to mean?" Barry shot back in a raised voice.

"Let's be frank, Mr. Stempler," Dr. Green explained, catching another sneeze before it had a chance, "your daughter appears to have rejected coming to you with her problems up to this point. And here you live in the same city."

Barry glared back at the doctor, his feet rocking beneath him like a prizefighter's. "You listen to me," he argued, his face beet red, "the woman's got one foot in the grave. She's ready for an institution herself."

Green leaned to his left, sizing up the fierce little woman gazing back at him, her eyes flashing determination. He looked again at Barry, assessing him as well. Then he turned back to check things out for himself.

"You'll forgive me, Mrs. . . ."

"Call me Gabby."

"Gabby. If she were to go with you you'd need to take responsibility for her 24/7. Can you do that?"

"I can handle the streets of New York,

Doctor. I think I can manage one sad young woman."

"She's more than sad. She's suicidal," Green corrected. "It won't be an easy task."

Gabby smiled with understanding. "Someone you love is suffering. It's not about easy, is it, Doctor?"

He searched her face and then nodded, impressed. It struck him that with the ward filled to overflowing, his staff overworked, and results often mixed, it was a gift to find an ally like this old woman. Having just lost a patient on the young man's second attempt following an extended hospitalization, Green was in the mood for alternatives. This old lady's feistiness reminded him that he had once idealized treating the soul, not just the symptoms. He was surrounded by bureaucracy, people wanting to shift responsibility. This grandmother stepping forward was like a drink of fresh water. And right there, Green decided to trust his gut. Of course he'd have to put it to the patient.

"Let's see what she has to say about it," he suddenly announced.

"I don't get it. What does that mean?" Barry demanded.

"It means we ask Jennifer." The doctor swiped at his nose with a handkerchief, staring into Gabby's eyes. "It's her life. Let's see if she cares enough to have an opinion about it."

A short time later Jennifer sat uncomfortably in a cramped consultation room facing Dr. Green across a table. She eyed her father at the end of the table to her left. He was whispering instructions to some no-doubt-harried assistant until Green's stern glance caused him to flip his phone closed, but he continued to fidget in his chair. At the other end of the table Gabby sat like a bundle of coiled energy, a crease in her forehead that she tried in vain to relax.

"As I explained to you in your room, Jennifer, your father has offered to foot the bill for a private facility where you might be more comfortable."

Jennifer looked over at her father. *You mean* he'd *be more comfortable,* she thought to herself and looked away.

"Your grandmother wants to take you back to New York to live with her for a short time. Get your feet back on the ground." Jennifer glanced quickly at Gabby, whose eyes were focused, birdlike.

"I won't dance around it, the staff wants to hold you. In that sense they side with your father. I'm the supervising physician, so it's my call."

A chill ran down Jennifer as she glared at Green. "Then what are we doing here?"

The doctor smiled, pushing his glasses back on his nose as he leaned forward. "I'd consider your release, but only if you are ready to make the commitment I would need."

Jennifer bit her lip and stared hard through the lone window. Worse than the thought of living was the idea that her father, and those who agreed with him, would control her destiny. Being locked up and having little visits from good old dad and his precious family held zero appeal. The prospect of enduring a series of family therapy meetings and further psych assessments was as unappetizing as it was pointless. She looked over at her nana, who struck her as a sweet little old lady, clearly without a clue. Jennifer's heart was racing. This was a no-brainer. But what was the price Green would demand?

"What would I have to do to go with *her?*" Jennifer blurted out.

Gabby slapped her hands together with excitement.

"Wait just a minute, Jennifer," Barry objected, rising in his seat.

"I'll handle this, Mr. Stempler, if you don't mind," the doctor asserted, his authoritative tone sending Barry angrily back into his seat.

"You would have to make a contract with me," Green answered, his face suddenly animated in a way Gabby hadn't seen earlier. "Tell me you have no intention of making another suicide attempt. Agree to faithfully take the antidepressants that will be provided. Remain under your grandmother's direct supervision. Check in with a licensed therapist while away. And agree to be back here for psychological assessment by Thanksgiving. That's six weeks from today. Now can you do that?" He paused. And before she could answer, he added with a measure of gravity, "Can you make me believe you will?"

The room held its breath. Jennifer cast a glance over at her father, who was muttering and shifting in his seat like a kid off his Ritalin. Clenching her fists under the table, Jennifer turned toward her nana. She saw the hopeful look filling Gabby's face. Something there reminded her of her mother, but Jennifer dismissed it like an unwanted provocation. She needed to focus on getting this doctor off her case. That was the business at hand. Digging down as deep as possible, Jennifer looked up at Green, and with every ounce of conviction she could muster, announced bravely, "You got it. Everything." Her face was suddenly flushed with sincerity, her tone that of someone who wanted desperately to heal, to get on with her life. "Being with my nana feels right. I want to move on. Believe me, Doctor."

The doctor held her gaze a moment, studying her. Her eyes were focused, vulnerable, hopeful. Slowly Green began to nod, agreeing. "All right, Jennifer. All right."

A hint of triumph flashed across Gabby's face.

"She's not in any position to go out there," Barry protested in the tone of a producer used to getting his way. "This must border on malpractice. What the hell do you think you're doing?"

"I'm giving your daughter a choice."

Green pulled out a sheet of paper and began writing up the agreement.

Barry turned and threw open the door, exiting in a huff. Green excused himself and followed him. He found Barry pacing the corridor like a caged animal.

"You don't get it, do you?" Barry muttered accusingly, still moving. "Look, I blew it with Jennifer, all right. I know it. She knows it. Damn it, Lili sure as hell knew it."

"Mr. Stempler," Green responded, offering a reassuring hand to the shoulder that

Barry instantly shook off as he passed by. "Beating yourself up isn't going to help you or your daughter at this point."

"No? This will just be one more time that somebody else is the good guy and I'm the asshole. I don't know the reasons she tried to take her life, but I'm sure I'm in there somewhere. I don't know how to wrap my brain around that. I'm not good with guilt."

Green uttered simply, "This isn't about you, Mr. Stempler, right?" He paused. "This is about Jennifer."

Barry gave him a dismissive glance, looking as if he were mounting an outburst. But for once in his life, he could find no ready retort. He stopped pacing and came to a standstill, exhaling sharply as the fight seeped out of him. Barry bit his lip, feeling the doctor's eyes on him as he gazed broodingly off into the distance. "Right," he uttered, powerless. "It's about Jennifer."

Later, after Green and Jennifer had drawn up and signed their contract, Jennifer was escorted back to her room and Green moved to speak with Gabby, Barry hanging on nearby.

"I'm going to have my office go over with you a list of things you'll need to remove from your home as a safety precaution. You've got just six weeks. I can't stress

36

strongly enough that she absolutely must be home by Thanksgiving for a thorough evaluation. You need to arrange psychological counseling for her, a minimum of once a week."

Handing her his card, Green impressed upon Gabby that the therapist must be state licensed and he would offer some recommendations. He promised to keep Barry informed of Jennifer's progress. When he was done, Gabby took the doctor's hands in her own.

"You've done a good thing here," she said with appreciation and warmth. Green smiled.

"Good luck to you, Mrs. . . ."

"Gabby."

"Right. Gabby." He added under his breath, "You get in over your head, you call me. Godspeed." She smiled back, her eyes twinkling. She was determined never to have to make such a call.

Barry interrupted, in motion again, grabbing for influence, "You'll need money for her therapy, clothes, I suppose, whatever." In charge again, Barry scribbled Gabby a sizable check on the spot. It was worth it. He knew his wife would breathe a sigh of relief that the buck had been passed.

As he handed the money to Gabby, Barry

looked her firmly in the eye and said, "I need you to deliver on this."

Gabby glanced up at him, restraining herself from saying something she'd regret. Something like "If you'd stuck it out with my daughter she might still be here. Things might be different. Jennifer might not have become lost." Instead, she took the check and stuck it in her pocketbook with a snap.

At the airport a few days later, Jennifer thought she caught a glimpse of a tear in her father's eye when he said his good-byes. He was uncharacteristically quiet, she noted, and for once wasn't bouncing all over the place. He just stood there staring at her, his trophy wife and their Kewpie doll of an infant alongside. For no apparent reason, it suddenly dawned on Jennifer that this little usurper she found so annoying was in fact related to her. This unsettling thought and her father's strange stillness was simply too bizarre and Jennifer excused herself and headed for the restroom. Gabby and the others waited uncomfortably just outside the door.

Jennifer turned the water on and stood in front of the mirror looking intently at herself. She hardly recognized the young woman looking back. Shaking her head, she took a deep breath and started to leave. Something made her pause before opening the door. Reaching into her tan leather jacket, she pulled out the contract she'd signed with Green. In the other pocket was a prescription for Prozac she'd been given to help her with her depression. She stared at them a moment. Here were her tickets of admission back into the world. She shrugged, crumpling the contract and the prescription in her hand, tossing them both into the wastebasket on her way out.

Aboard the plane, Jennifer gazed out her window as the aircraft rose over Venice Beach. Her stomach became twisted in knots. She peered down at the ocean, its waters dappled in the morning sunlight. With the speed of the jet, she felt as if she were skating at a maddening clip along the water's surface. She suddenly felt nauseated and turned to find her nana coughing forcefully into a handkerchief. How old she had become, how frail, Jennifer thought. Since Lili's death, Gabby had wanted to help, wanted to reach out to comfort her granddaughter and herself. But Jennifer hadn't allowed that to happen. She found herself now trying to remember exactly why. Had it been because Gabby reminded her so much of her mom? she wondered. Or could it have been the love Gabby had seemed almost desperate to share and that Jennifer had been just as desperate to escape?

It was all about the pain, Jennifer reminded herself. Which is exactly the reason she had decided it was best to simply shut out everyone who mattered. Now she found herself asking why this delicate, clearly ailing woman didn't do the same. Why would she want to take on someone whose life was so utterly and completely a nightmare, someone who in fact might be closer to death than she was?

Coincidentally, Gabby, who out of the corner of her eye had been studying the lump of grief her granddaughter had become, was asking herself the very same thing.

5

As the lights in the Midtown Tunnel flicked overhead, Jennifer stared at the smothering, gritty walls flying by the window. She hadn't uttered a word since landing at Kennedy. Gabby had been talking nonstop about a new play she was sure Jennifer would love. Then there was the Leonardo da Vinci exhibit at the Met that was a masterpiece of genius and observation, and they would definitely want to go to a concert at Carnegie Hall. What is it with her? Jennifer said to herself. Does she work for the freakin' chamber of commerce?

Reflected in the glass, her nana's mouth was still moving, but Jennifer had tuned out the sound. Queasy from the ride, she steadied herself against the metal and plastic partition that separated them from the driver, Gabby's monologue continuing in the background.

". . . and then we can always take the subway to Coney Island. One time . . ."

As the nausea subsided, Jennifer noticed the cabdriver's white turban. As the cab stopped for a light, Jennifer stared out at the weather-beaten face of a homeless man encased in a ripped-up old sleeping bag, drinking something from a paper bag as he lay on a bench by the corner. Car horns blared around her and the loud thump of a stereo system in the gold-plated Benz next to them rattled everything that wasn't nailed down.

Gabby had paused, taking in the catatonic creature to her right. She then turned to address the driver.

"I bet where you come from you speak to your grandparents when they talk to you? Isn't that right?" Gabby leaned forward, squinting to make out the driver's name on the ID badge hanging from the glove compartment. "Mr. Tambori, is it?"

"Yes, can I help you?" the driver responded in his clipped Indian accent.

Gabby repeated herself as Jennifer rolled her eyes, shaking her head. At least it was *some* reaction.

The cab lurched to the right to avoid a sports car that had darted into traffic, sending Gabby crashing into her ward. Gabby managed to pull herself back and Jennifer righted herself, too.

"That was nothing. Listen, you remember the blizzard of '96," Gabby went on between coughs and wheezing, "you couldn't stay on the road. Cars were skating down Fifth Avenue. I don't think my granddaughter has ever seen anything like that," Gabby blared, getting louder as she rambled on. "She's from California. I'm going to give her a crash course in the wildlife of Central Park, however. *Be-you-tee-ful* this time of year. Am I right, Mr. Tambori?"

Jennifer wished her nana came with a Pause button.

"Look at these people, Mr. Tambori," Gabby declared, practically yelling as she pointed out her window. "Racing here and there. They don't even see each other, I'm sure of it."

The driver looked into his rearview mirror, rolling his eyes as he caught Jennifer's gaze. Jennifer nodded slightly and looked away. She spied a worker plying a jackhammer on the street, wasting away everything in his path. The sound grew louder and louder, drowning out the voice of her grandmother as bits of gravel and cement spat out in all directions.

They turned on 69th Street between Columbus and Central Park West. "Thank God," Gabby muttered as the cab finally pulled up in front of her aging brownstone. She had to coax Jennifer out of the vehicle.

As the driver removed their bags from the trunk, Gabby offered him a nice tip to take them up the steps and inside the front door.

Jennifer stood on the sidewalk, staring up at the unimposing five-story building before her. There was a hint of its former grandeur in the façade. Placed outside each window were unadorned flower boxes whose contents needed tending. A large frieze of a Greek laurel wreath was prominent along floors three and four. At the entrance was a short stoop with a railing that looked to be newly painted. Its fresh appearance, however, was spoiled by disrepair, a section having cracked away, where it hung off to the side without purpose.

Across the street Jennifer observed a driver trying in vain to park her SUV in a space half the size needed. Suddenly her brain jumped with activity. It was the story of her life. She simply couldn't wedge herself into a space in life where circumstances out of her control had left her no room. It was like being in a crowded pool where she couldn't float freely. What in the hell was she doing here with Nana anyway? What would Gabby be able to do with her special brand of darkness? This whole thing was absurd. Jennifer's heart beat wildly. Maybe her father was right. She had overheard him telling his wife that Jennifer belonged in a facility somewhere. Maybe she could get the driver to take her back to the airport? Or maybe she could simply disappear, make sure this time that the deed was done? "Move, Jennifer. *Run!*" she told herself.

Yet her legs would not obey. Instead, she stood immobile, her head full of questions and self-recrimination. Slowly she became aware that her nana's eyes were on her. As the cab pulled away, Gabby nodded back at her as if she could discern everything going on inside Jennifer at that moment.

"Don't be afraid, sheyna meydele," she said. "I'll take care of you until you get your strength. We'll find our way together, you'll see. Come."

Then, taking hold of her granddaughter's hand, Gabby led her up the stoop and into her world.

6

Memories washed over Jennifer as she stood in the entranceway to the World War I era apartment. Having made but a handful of visits here, she nevertheless remembered well the cramped layout of the place and what as a child she called its "Nana smell." She immediately saw a picture of her mother as a young girl. Lili was standing by the sea, hands raised in triumph. *How happy she was then,* Jennifer thought. Jennifer recalled trips down to the shore with her mother to chase sunsets along the ocean. Sunset, for Lili, was the magical time of day when, as she liked to say, "heaven and earth kissed." Jennifer would stand on her mother's feet at the boundary of sand and sea, the two of them delighting as the salt water, shimmering with the last vestiges of light, flowed cold and bubbly around their toes.

Jennifer had a faint recollection of an older man, glasses askew, chasing her through the rooms as she giggled. Putting down her bag, Jennifer moved from the narrow vestibule down the long central hallway, its walls covered in family photographs of all shapes and sizes.

As Jennifer paused to examine the black-and-white photo of a young couple dancing along a waterfront, Gabby looked on from a distance. Jennifer drew nearer, studying the faces of the man and the woman in the picture. He was handsome with a ruddy complexion that reflected his love of the outdoors. There was a life in his eyes, a passion. Something about the way his mouth was open, as if he were roaring at the world, reminded Jennifer a little of Phillip. She gasped at the pain of that memory. She looked now at the smiling woman in the photo. She was dressed in a colorful evening dress in the style of half a century ago, turning on a single foot as the man held her outstretched hand. She looked like the princess at the ball, one who has just found her prince. Jennifer glanced back at the man twirling his partner. She had been two when her grandfather, whom she called Papa, had died, leaving Gabby a widow while still in her fifties. The first of many to bite the dust, Jennifer quipped to herself. Phillip had once said he would grow old with her, hadn't he? Like her father, he was the sort of man who promised a lot of things he didn't deliver.

Continuing down the dark hallway, Jennifer dragged a hand haphazardly across the antique oak table as she passed through the modest kitchen leading into the living room. The furniture there was an eclectic mix of styles and patterns, but comfy all the same. Jennifer suddenly remembered having taken the subway to Brighton Beach to visit some friends of her nana's when she was little. She recalled the funny odor, as if the apartment had been hung in mothballs. But it was the furniture that really made an impression. Each cushion, couch, and pillow was sheathed in plastic like food in the freezer. She had been only seven at the time, but it didn't stop Jennifer from piping up that "someone needs to take off the plastic bags so the chairs don't crackle-crackle." This remark had caused the butterball of a hostess to gasp, "Remove the plastic? God forbid!" Jennifer, Lili, and Gabby had laughed all the way back to Manhattan.

Gabby, who had allowed Jennifer a little space to get her bearings, now showed her how the couch could be pulled out into a full-sized sofa bed, where she could sleep. Jennifer took a deep breath and exhaled, looking over at the glass coffee table over-flowing with her nana's collection of tchotchkes. It was as if she'd entered a time warp, fallen into some kind of black hole where everything modern and contemporary had ceased to exist.

After unpacking, Jennifer opted for a hot shower while Gabby phoned Barry. Though her relationship with the man who had walked out on her daughter had scarcely been civil ever since the divorce, it now seemed to Gabby that, under the circumstances, calling him was the right thing to do. Despite his many less-than-stellar qualities, Barry was still Jennifer's father, and Gabby respected the role, if not the man filling it. Nevertheless, she would rather have talked to a porcupine and was relieved when she got his voice mail: "It's Barry. I'm either on the set or closing a deal. Hey, that's Hollywood. You know the drill. Ciao."

"Hi there, Barry. It's us," Gabby said, sounding decidedly upbeat. "Wanted you to know we arrived just fine. Fine. Everything's good and . . . fine. Jennifer is just beside herself, really, with excitement, I guess. Actually, she's speechless really, what with being in the Big Apple. Anyway, not to worry. We're having a big night out on the town. Two ladies loose on the city. All right now, regards to the family. Oh, this is Gabby. 'Bye."

That night they ordered Chinese take-out, and with Jennifer muttering few words and barely touching her food, Gabby decided it best they turn in early. Gabby helped Jennifer unroll and prepare the sofa bed, discussing plans to go to a Broadway musical the next day "just to let our hair down."

"Why do anything?" Jennifer suddenly interjected.

For a moment, Gabby was taken aback and had to close her eyes to fight the anger. If only Lili were still alive, they could all go together. And if Itzik had been around, he would know what to do with this selfish ingrate of a granddaughter. Her mind turned back to thoughts of her sister, Anna, who had been eight years younger than Jennifer when she died. Gabby stifled a heavy cough. Turning out the lights, she sat next to the girl on the sofa bed. Studying Jennifer — silent, closed off, and helpless — Gabby was suddenly overwhelmed with emotion. She felt so alone. Anna, Itzik, Lili — gone. Jennifer was all that was left of her family, her lifeline to everyone else. And despite everything the young woman was putting her through, Gabby loved her more than life itself. If only Jennifer could feel that somehow.

She reached out a hand to brush a lock of hair from Jennifer's forehead. This time Jennifer did not retreat but simply allowed it to happen. And then, as she had done for Lili, and Lili in turn for Jennifer, Gabby put her granddaughter to sleep with a lullaby in the language of her youth: "Shlof, myn tokhter, sheyna, fayne." *Sleep, my good pretty daughter, sleep.* Gabby sang until Jennifer had drifted off for the night.

Later, worn to the bone from travel and the strain of settling in her new roommate, Gabby lay awake running the situation she faced through her mind. It was the tenth of October. The way things stood, she had until Thanksgiving to shake her granddaughter to life. After that, Barry would make it impossible for her to hold on to Jennifer. Indeed, Dr. Green, for all his support, was adamant about Jennifer's return. If Gabby failed to bring Jennifer back from the brink she would no doubt be placed in some facility and face a life of institutionalized God knows what. Barry had let Gabby know as much at the airport, slipping her some extra cash while whispering about a court order if Gabby failed to have his daughter back so that he could get her some "real" help.

Suddenly questions she had refused to

consider popped into her head. What if Barry was right? What if Jennifer tried suicide again while under her care? Gabby's heart began to beat faster. What if her granddaughter actually succeeded in slipping away, how would she ever live with herself? She wouldn't. Gabby closed her eyes tight as if to ward off these thoughts.

Remembering the list of drugs Green had given her in the hospital, she got up and removed all of the medicine bottles from the bathroom cabinet, even the suppositories. She hadn't the slightest idea what medications could be put in what orifices, and you couldn't be too careful. It was best to do away with all possible temptation.

After locking up the prescription medicines she absolutely needed for her own use, Gabby had gone around and collected any instruments that had sharp edges — scissors, cutting utensils, sewing needles — stashing them in an old hatbox in the closet. She kept out her silverware knives, figuring Jennifer might feel self-conscious if forced to cut her food with a spoon and fork.

At a moment like this most people might turn to their faith. But Gabby had maintained a love-hate relationship with God ever since the war. He had failed to come to her family's aid when they needed Him the most in Poland, and as far as she was concerned, there was absolutely no excuse for that. Nevertheless, in moments of joy, such as when she and Itzik got married, and when her daughter and granddaughter were born, Gabby found herself offering up a prayer of gratitude.

Given the crisis she now faced, however, the God she had come to know didn't seem a reliable bet. No, the situation with Jennifer was too important to leave to a rank amateur who seemed to show up on a whim one day and disappear the next. "Lili," Gabby called out softly, "you always knew what to do when it came to Jennifer. She's been lost ever since you left us. So, sweetheart, talk to me. You got any ideas?"

She fell into a fitful sleep, still waiting for a reply.

7

Gabby woke with a start. But as she caught sight of the figure sitting at the foot of her bed she was certain she must be dreaming. It couldn't be, could it? There was Lili, just as she used to be as a child, patiently waiting for her mother to wake up so they could start their day. Only she didn't appear as a little girl, nor was she forty-four, the age at which she had been tragically killed in an accident. Rather she was a young woman again and she was here alive in Gabby's bedroom! Heart racing with disbelief, Gabby reached for her glasses on the bedside table. Placing them on, she looked up to find Jennifer staring back at her, her face creased with puzzled detachment.

"You surprised me. I thought for a moment I'm going a little crazy." A self-conscious laugh spilled from her lips as she realized her choice of words might not have been the best. "Is anything wrong? Did you have a bad dream?"

"No," Jennifer replied matter-of-factly.

"Actually, I don't think I dreamt at all," she shrugged. "I don't remember."

Gabby nodded, getting her bearings. "How long have you been sitting there?"

"I don't know . . . ten minutes, half an hour," Jennifer responded drily, glancing around the room as if she had just discovered it and wondered how she had come to be there.

"I'm not as beautiful sleeping as I am when I'm awake, am I?" Gabby quipped, reaching for her bathrobe, determined to get the day on track. "Come, let's have some breakfast. How does Nana's matza brei sound?"

Jennifer followed her into the kitchen, pausing in the doorway as if she wasn't sure she was supposed to enter. Gabby stole a glance at her while lighting the burner. Jennifer didn't appear to be angry or even as distant as she had been yesterday. It was more as if she had awakened suspended in a fog.

"How come I'm here, Nana?" Jennifer abruptly asked in the simple tone of one with amnesia. Gabby wondered at the strange question. But from the honest bewilderment on her granddaughter's face it was clear Jennifer was truly laboring to piece it all together.

Gabby placed the butter in the pan and

reached for a box of matza in the cupboard above the small counter, never taking her eyes off her granddaughter.

"You're here to get better, meydele," Gabby replied, as if it were a foregone conclusion.

Jennifer thought about that for a moment, attempting to decipher her nana's response. The sound of butter sizzling filled the air. She watched Gabby crack several eggs, whip them with a fork, adding a bit of pepper and salt and a pinch of cinnamon before crumbling pieces of matza into the mixture.

"Nana," she suddenly asked blankly, as one might inquire about the weather, "what's wrong with me?"

Gabby stopped what she was doing, grabbing the corners of her apron as if to anchor herself. She felt as if her heart would break. She struggled not to give too much weight to her answer.

"You lost your way, little one," she replied evenly, adding a reassuring smile as she poured the mixture into the frying pan. "And together we're going to help you find it."

Then Jennifer asked another question for which Gabby was totally unprepared. "Does she know I'm here?"

"Who?"

"My mother."

Gabby stopped what she was doing and stared at the pan in front of her. Turning off the burner, she wiped her hands on the apron and walked over to the doorway where Jennifer was still standing, shifting on the balls of her feet.

"Jennifer, you're under so much pressure right now. Maybe we shouldn't —"

"I tried to kill myself, right?" Jennifer blurted out with cool detachment, as if the memory had just clicked into place.

Gabby led her over to the antique kitchen table, sat her down, and pulled a chair up alongside her. "Yes, sheyna," Gabby said softly.

Jennifer began running it through her mind as if she were solving a puzzle for which she had too many pieces.

"They found me there on the beach. They found me there and I didn't finish, I didn't get to . . ." Her words dropped off as she stared into space, remembering the scene.

Gabby studied the troubled face of her granddaughter. It was as if the night had erased her memory and she was only now recovering the horrible truth of her actions. Or was she attempting to fathom how it had all gone wrong? Did she want to try it again? Gabby knew it was dangerous to let Jennifer dwell on the event. Having experienced horror in her own life, she knew there was a time for memory and a time for doing anything else *but* remember. This was one of those times. She needed to change the focus, to disrupt the scene. But how?

And then, as if she'd heard a whisper in her soul, it came to her. With a sudden burst, Gabby clapped her hands eagerly together.

"Do you know what we're going to do today?" she blurted out, interrupting Jennifer's trance. Like a child about to embark on an adventure, Gabby spoke in a voice filled with energy. She grabbed her granddaughter's hand with an electrifying firmness.

"We are going to eat this matza brei, which we all know to be the world's finest, and don't tell me different, Jennifer, because you know it's the truth," she declared all in one breath, "and then we are going to go over to the stables in the park." She paused, eyes twinkling with mischief.

Jennifer shook her head. "The stables?" she asked.

8

"You want to do what?" the boss at Central Park's Claremont Stables roared. "Look, lady, this is a serious operation we run here. You don't waltz in from the street offering to clean up horseshit. That's nuts!"

"Why not? You've got it. We want to shovel it," Gabby said matter-of-factly.

"Well, because it's just not done. I mean, what kind of crazy person — excuse my language — wants to come in here and toss horse manure into a wheelbarrow? Whoever heard of a thing like that?"

"You just heard of it," Gabby responded with a cockeyed little grin, heading for the center of the riding ring.

The stable boss and Jennifer stood side by side, bewildered.

"What's with this woman anyway?" he muttered to Jennifer, shaking his head at the audacity of it all.

Nonplussed, Jennifer stared at her grandmother and shrugged. "I don't know. She's from the old country," she said with detachment. "I guess she really misses her horses."

Gabby had already taken up a shovel in the corner of the indoor riding ring, wielding it with determined grit. The stable boss stood back, folded his arms, and grinned, deciding he was going to enjoy this. Jennifer stood motionless, gaping at her nana hoisting a load of manure into a wheelbarrow. She then reached for her camcorder and turned it on. After several swings of the shovel, however, Gabby paused and leaned on the implement, fixing her granddaughter with an all-business squint.

"Forgive me, but what's wrong with this picture?" Gabby challenged, cocking her head. "I am a seventy-six-year-old woman with bad lungs. You, my darling granddaughter, are all of twenty-three. We're not sightseeing today. So put down the camera, get your tush over here, and give me a hand already."

Speechless, Jennifer obeyed. The stable boss began corralling others to witness the sight of the two women working in the ring. They kept at it diligently for several minutes, each watching the other perform her task. Jennifer couldn't stop shaking her head in disbelief that she and her grandmother were undertaking so ridiculous an enter-

prise. Yet somewhere inside her was an in-
kling of admiration at the sheer chutzpah of
it all. She and Gabby emptied their shovels
again and again. Then, out of nowhere,
Jennifer felt a glob of horseshit hit her leg.
Looking up, astounded, she saw her nana
grinning.

"Oops, sorry there, darling, I missed,"
Gabby offered in mock innocence.

Jennifer's eyes narrowed. She studied
Gabby, who continued her work while
stealing mischievous glances up at her
granddaughter. Jennifer shook her head.
This lady is nuts, she told herself. She returned to her own efforts but immediately
was struck with another stinking glob.
Calmly Jennifer lifted more manure into the
wheelbarrow; then with a mighty grunt, she
let fly a shovelful, making a direct hit on her
nana's feet. Jennifer shrugged, her smile sly,
as Gabby eyed her with suspicion. In the
next instant Jennifer got lobbed with more
shit. Suddenly the gloves were off. Quickly
the situation dissolved as the pair began
flinging manure back and forth. They were
firing volleys at will, struggling to hit their
target, slinging the stuff over the wheelbarrow at each other with what could only
be called passion.

Pausing, Gabby stood back, staring into

Jennifer's suddenly lively eyes. The two fought to catch their breath. As Gabby coughed up some phlegm and cleared her throat like a wizened old cowboy, she could swear she saw in Jennifer's suddenly flashing eyes the spark of emotion she craved. The girl was having — could it be — a little fun?

The stable boss and the few workers who had enjoyed the impromptu show grinned widely, pitching in to shovel up the mess. Exhausted, slightly giddy, Jennifer and Gabby thanked them and stumbled for the exit.

"You, uh . . . ladies have yourselves a good day," the boss called after them, shaking his head and roaring with laughter.

After cleaning themselves up, Gabby and Jennifer set out for a stroll through the park and some much needed fresh air. But exposure to the dust in the stables had irritated Gabby's lungs, and before long she was doubled over hacking, an episode that forced her to a nearby bench. Jennifer stood by, observing her nana convulsively coughing. She felt the impulse to move toward her grandmother, but the message never reached her legs as she watched the tortured old woman gasping. These painful sounds attracted a couple passing by. They stared accusingly at the young woman and offered Gabby their assistance. The episode soon passed and Gabby thanked the couple. They moved on, shooting one more aggrieved glance in Jennifer's direction. There was a long pause as Gabby sat back on the park bench composing herself. She slowly looked up at her granddaughter, her grin restored.

"Wasn't that disgusting?"

"Your coughing?" Jennifer remarked.

"What coughing? Shoveling all that crap back there."

Jennifer couldn't help but crack a smile. "Yeah, really disgusting."

Gabby closed her eyes a moment, nodding. "But fun, am I right?"

Jennifer considered that, pursing her lips. "I suppose . . . in a really sick kind of way," she allowed.

"How many granddaughters do you suppose can say they shoveled horse poop with their nanas even once in their life?"

Jennifer nodded halfheartedly, finally reaching out to help Gabby to her feet.

It was later, while they were sitting eating hot dogs in the Sheep Meadow, that Gabby turned to her and said, "Of course she knows you're here."

Jennifer looked up, distracted, swiping

her tongue at the mustard at the corner of her mouth. "What are you talking about?"

"You asked me this morning if your mother knows you're here, Jennifer, and I'm answering you. Yes, absolutely, one thousand percent."

Jennifer paused, putting down her hot dog. She picked up her camcorder and began filming the white puffs of clouds dotting the sky overhead. Gabby watched her curiously.

"You're going to keep carrying that thing everywhere?" she asked.

Jennifer's eyes never left the eyepiece. "You want to see the real world, you have to shut out all the distractions. It's a matter of focus. Most people only think they see what's going on."

Gabby started to speak but decided it best not to challenge.

It wasn't just about focus, Jennifer told herself. Recording events meant time could be stopped, played back, even erased.

Jennifer put the camera down. She appeared to be turning something over in her head and Gabby wanted to give whatever it was the time to surface.

After a few moments, Jennifer spoke, in a low, distant voice. "It happened so fast, you know?" She paused, looking down as if deciding to continue and then gazing off to her right. Gabby followed her eyes to where two toddlers were playing with a striped beach ball while their nannies looked on.

"I never expected it, never expected her to leave me that way. The guy swore he'd never been drunk in his life. You believe that? Lost his job, wife left. So, what the hell, right? Get behind the wheel and take somebody out." She leaned her head back and exhaled. "Seventeen other people were crossing that street and every single one of them lived. He manages to find my mother."

Gabby closed her eyes, remembering the heartrending shock of that phone call informing her of the tragic accident that had taken her daughter.

"I was using her car that day 'cause mine was in the shop. The brakes were shot, Mom's cards were maxed out. My dad hadn't given Mom any money for a long time. Bad investments, he said. Whatever he gave us, she used on me. I asked if he could cover the brakes and he insisted on arranging for his mechanic to do the work. Like usual, it wasn't one of his top priorities. Mom offered me her car that day to be sure I'd get to exams on time. She said she could walk. She liked walking." Her voice trailed off.

"I remember," Gabby said softly, closing her eyes.

Jennifer looked around. "She had this book in her hands she'd just bought me. *Oh, the Places You'll Go!* by Dr. Seuss. For my graduation." Off to the right one of the toddlers started crying. Jennifer glanced over and then away again.

"The book — this is the amazing thing — it made it. Survived the crash. I mean, there was hardly any dirt on it, it wasn't torn or anything. And there was this inscription inside she must have written in the store."

"I didn't know this," Gabby interjected, transfixed.

" 'To my beautiful daughter,' it said, 'who is learning to reach beyond the stars to where dreams are real.' " She broke off and buried her head in her hands.

Gabby's lips trembled. She could hear Lili's voice speaking these words.

Suddenly Jennifer's head shot up. She stared intensely at her nana, narrowing her eyes. Gabby could see now they were filled with pain and fury.

"That's not why I did it, you know? It wasn't like my mother got killed and I was all 'poor little me' and five years later, *boom,* I go for it. You know that, right, Nana? I mean, people don't think I did this because of her?"

"What do you care what people think, meydele?" Gabby said softly. "What matters is only what *you* think."

Jennifer grew silent. She watched the toddlers being put in their strollers and wheeled away from the meadow. She played with the remainder of her hot dog a moment before throwing it in the vicinity of a Dalmatian whose owner was walking it through the park.

"You want to know why I never called you before taking the pills, don't you?" Jennifer said, pursing her lips, her tone confrontational.

"I am a little curious, I admit, Jennifer. But you don't have to . . ."

"Because you would have done exactly what you did just now, come flying across the country to stop me. You know I'm right about that."

Gabby smiled, nodding. "Would that have been so bad? To stop you from giving up on life?"

"Yes!" Jennifer shot back immediately, startling Gabby. "I couldn't let someone stop me because it is the only way I can control things. Don't you see that? It wasn't about giving up then or now. That thinking is so yesterday. No, it was a decision. *My* decision."

Gabby had grown increasingly unsettled, fearing that Jennifer might run off. She wanted to say something to reach her, to hold her, but simply waited. Jennifer didn't move but rather sat there, rubbing her face vigorously as if to wipe away the memory of those who had thwarted her intentions. Finally Gabby coughed several times, caught her breath, and began to speak with a strength belying her apparent frailness.

"You believed it was your duty to end the life that your mother, my daughter of blessed memory, gave you. I believe it is my duty to show you that you're wrong. I'm listening to *her* voice now. 'Mama,' she says, 'save my little girl for me. I would do it myself, but she doesn't seem to hear me. So you, Mama, you must act, please!' "

Gabby studied Jennifer, afraid that she might drive her away and terrified at the same time of the consequences of remaining silent.

"You say you want control," Gabby went on. "Control is what I prayed for every day I hid in Poland. The chance to take control of my own life rather than have my destiny in the hands of monsters."

"Please, Nana, not the Holocaust speech," Jennifer shot back with agitation, looking away. Gabby did her best to remain calm, taking a deep breath before responding quietly.

"Yes, Jennifer, the Holocaust speech. And I will give it again and again until I have no breath in my body. Until you hear the voice of that little girl who was your nana, who every night wanted only to scream 'More life!' at a God who could not hear her amid all the killing."

She paused, catching her breath. "But no one listened to me then, just as you believe no one can hear you now, am I right?"

Gabby scooted closer to Jennifer, who drew back, keeping her distance.

"It was an accident that I returned from the dead, just like it was with you." She paused a moment, searching for a response but getting none. "Sometimes we need to take advantage of life's accidents, yes? So" — Gabby rose and brushed herself off — "come, let's go home."

Jennifer looked up at her with resentment. "I don't have to stay here. You can't force me, you know?"

"That's correct." Gabby sighed. "But your father will hire men to come and find you and bring you back and put you in some institution. I would hate to see that happen to you, Jennifer." Gabby turned away, feeling the effects of this strain but determined to have her say. Then she rounded on Jennifer with one more thought.

"I realize you could also threaten to run off and hurt yourself again. But it is no answer to the hurt that is in your heart. Besides, darling," she added with an impish twinkle of her eye, "it would be a horrible thing to do to an old woman who just this morning introduced you to the joys of shoveling horse poop, am I right?"

Gabby held her breath and stared at her granddaughter, who sat unmoved, expressionless. Gabby looked away. There was silence. And then a reply.

"Shit."

"What's that?" Gabby coughed, caught off guard by the word and by the fact that Jennifer had said anything at all.

Jennifer just shook her head. "Not *poop*, Nana. Nobody calls it *poop*. It's horse*shit*. If I can shovel it, you can call it by its name. Go ahead." She stared up at her grandmother, a challenge in her eyes.

"You want me to . . ." Gabby laughed uncomfortably, shaking her head.

But Jennifer wasn't moving. Glancing

from side to side, God forbid anyone else should hear, Gabby spoke softly. "All right," she offered with a giggle. "Shhhh . . . i . . . t."

"No, no, that's no good," Jennifer shot back, shaking her head dismissively. "You're not getting by with that. Try it again. Really let one rip. Like this." Jennifer threw her head back and shouted, "Shit!" Gabby worried for a moment that someone might be listening. She glanced around at the Sheep Meadow with its lunchtime assembly of business workers, joggers, and tourists. And then, shrugging, she told herself, "Who cares what anyone else thinks?"

Bracing herself, Gabby opened her mouth. "Sh . . . it," she rasped in a somewhat louder, slightly wavering voice.

Despite herself, Jennifer smiled. Why was it so hard for people of a certain generation to curse? "Oh, come on. From the gut, Nana, you can do it."

"Shit" came the response in a voice that would barely disturb a bird.

"At least give it a little attitude!" Jennifer urged, enthusiastic now, bending over, hands on her knees, calling out encouragement. The two of them were now attracting the attention of a few curious onlookers.

"Sh-it!" Gabby called out.

"All right, all right, two syllables, but

we're getting somewhere. Put 'em together. You can do it," Jennifer prodded.

The old woman clenched her fists. "Shit!" she blurted out, looking at her grand-daughter expectantly.

"Give me more!"

"Shit!"

"More!"

"*Shit!*" came the bolder response. Gabby was genuinely excited by that attempt.

"That's it."

"Shit. Shit. *Shit!*" Gabby popped off.

"Put your body and soul into it, Nana. Go for the big one!" And with Jennifer encouraging with a manic urgency, Gabby stood in the popular gathering place with its lunchtime crowd and let loose with an astounding cry of "SHIT!" Cheers erupted. The people in the meadow responded with "You go, girl!" Gabby had completely blocked out the public. But now, becoming aware again of being heard, she fled the scene, dragging an amused Jennifer behind her.

The two collapsed just outside the gate, out of breath.

"Congratulations," Jennifer said wryly. "You are a goddamn disturber of the peace, you know that?"

"Well," Gabby shot back, gasping to catch her breath, eyes twinkling at the thought, "that might be true, lady, but you are a shoveler of horseshit."

Jennifer allowed herself a good laugh and Gabby thought finally, finally, the cloud of sadness had lifted. But as they walked on, Jennifer turned quiet, that awful darkness settling over her features again. Gabby witnessed this in silence, saddened by the transformation.

Jennifer lifted the camcorder and turned it on a dog growling nearby. Slowly she pulled in closer, focusing ever more tightly on the animal's angry eyes until its owner spoke sharply to the dog and it settled back.

Gabby wished she would put the contraption down. *The world isn't in that damn lens,* she cried out silently. *You're so busy focusing, Jennifer, only you're missing everything that really matters.*

9

Late that night Jennifer stood in the bathroom filming her reflection in the mirror. "It's like I've been kidnapped by an alien lifeform, only it's my grandmother." She paused, staring through the lens. "She is possibly certifiable." She thought for a second, then laughed self-consciously. "Look who's talking, right?"

Jennifer lowered the camera and took in her image in the mirror. Her eyes searched the face looking back at her.

The camcorder continued to record as she placed it on the counter and then slowly began to undress. She peeled off her sweater and then the T-shirt under it. Stepping out of her sweatpants and underwear, Jennifer undid her bra and faced herself in the mirror. She examined her body as a scientist might examine a specimen in the laboratory — clinically and with detachment.

She observed herself for several minutes. Then, reaching down, she picked up the framed photo of her grandparents she'd brought into the bathroom from the hallway. Jennifer propped it up against the mirror and studied it as if for the first time. Her grandmother and grandfather danced on forever in the photo. Delicately Jennifer stretched out her arm as if being twirled by her partner. Mirroring her nana's younger self, she slowly pirouetted once without emotion. She next touched the figures in the photo as if her fingers might capture the joy upon their faces.

Gazing back up at the mirror, she wrapped her arms around her naked body and stared back at the image of the fragile being who stood before her.

Letting out a deep breath, Jennifer switched off the camcorder, turned on the shower, and stepped in, lifting her face into the water pouring down on her head.

10

Gabby kept Jennifer busy that first week. They had taken in two plays and an IMAX presentation called *The Wonder of the Land Down Under* that had Gabby enthralled, though Jennifer had conked out before the title sequence was over. Twice they had come home to messages from Jennifer's father on Gabby's answering machine.

"Gabby, I insist on a phone call by the end of the day. The deal was for you to keep me updated. That was made perfectly clear. You've got my cell number. Use it." Put off by the tone, Gabby deliberately phoned his home when she knew he'd be out, letting Cynthia know all was well. The next day Barry responded with a rather patronizing message.

"It's not too much to ask, is it, a simple call on my cell phone? Even the script girl can get that right. I want to know what's going on. Don't shut me out. Let me remind you who's bankrolling this little experiment. I'm warning you . . ." That was it. Gabby flicked it off immediately. Now he'd gone too far. She had never liked warnings. Never even read a warning label. She'd call him back when she was ready. She couldn't deal with Barry's guilt, not with her hands full already.

Gabby was aware she was procrastinating when it came to locating a therapist for Jennifer and couldn't explain to herself quite why. A phone call from Dr. Green, however, finally set her into action. Midway through the second week, the doctor called and wanted to know how Jennifer was managing. He pointedly asked for the name of the psychologist Jennifer was now seeing. Gabby insisted the therapist's card was not handy and that she was on her way out. She assured the doctor, however, that she would call back soon with the information and that Jennifer was showing definite signs of progress.

The problem seemed to solve itself when the next day Gabby dragged a reluctant granddaughter to the apartment of her longtime friend, Frieda Steinberg, over on West End and 89th. Frieda was what Gabby referred to as a yenta friend. She lived to share gossip, both good and bad, and otherwise had a healthy appetite for knowing what's what. If it came down to choosing

CNN or Frieda as a reliable source of information, Gabby wouldn't give the cable network a second thought. Years back, when their husbands were both living, the two couples often double-dated to the theater or dancing at Roseland.

"C'mon, Gabby, old girl," Frieda would cry out on the dance floor, with a laugh as big as she was, "shake the leg God gave you and show these kids what cutting the rug is all about!" Their husbands had died within a year of each other, and Frieda and Gabby often found themselves in each other's company over a game of canasta or bridge, Frieda's more sedentary choices, or a walk in the park or a new play, Gabby's preferences. The two widows shared a love of good food and, before Jennifer's arrival, had met at least once a week at Zabar's for a talk and a nosh.

Frieda had pulled out all the stops for her visitors, putting out some cold borscht, meat knishes, chopped liver, a nice roast chicken and potatoes, a little schmaltz for dipping, along with a fresh loaf of pumpernickel and some two cents plain. Jennifer nibbled while the two women went at the spread like veterans. After as much small talk as Jennifer could stomach — details of the sales at Filene's and of Frieda's argument with her landlord over his refusal to put a fresh coat of paint on her front door despite a year's worth of promises, not to mention a list of who had died and left what to whom — she excused herself, holing up in the bathroom for some much-needed *space*.

If she had really wanted to cut her life short, she told herself, she should have moved to New York and hung out with Gabby's friends. The cholesterol alone would have done her in. In a habit she developed when Phillip had once stated "You know a person from the stuff they keep over the bathroom sink," Jennifer opened Frieda's medicine cabinet and perused its contents. Like her nana's, the cabinet was stocked with old-lady things: a jar of denture cleaner, an old, crusty bottle of cough medicine, a few wrinkled and tatty tubes of ointment, a veritable tub of petroleum jelly — what was she greasing with all this stuff? Moving jars and tubes aside, Jennifer found a funny-looking bottle of what appeared to be facial cream, its label written in a foreign language; an assortment of tweezers; and a veritable pharmacy of brown plastic vials: prescriptions for eczema and for the heart, iron supplements, and two little containers of Valium, one half empty, the other chock full.

Back at the deli in the kitchen, Gabby was discussing with Frieda her pressing problem of locating a suitable therapist.

"She's on this antidepressant, this Prozac, which she swears she's taking each day, but I don't see it doing much. I gave my word to this doctor she'd see someone. But who? To me, they're all the same, these shrinks."

"*Psychologists,* Gabby, darling, and I've got the answer to your prayers," replied Frieda, her face aglow with the enthusiasm normally reserved for food.

She nearly spilled over with praise for a Dr. Larry Nevins. Apparently he had worked wonders with her nephew's son Seth, who had got himself into serious trouble using — Frieda lowered her head, mouthing the word — "Cocaine." She swore up and down that Gabby could not go wrong giving him a call "if he'll even see you. The man's booked up, I understand, from here to God knows when." Gabby cut her off, however, when Jennifer decided to rejoin them. Frieda immediately pushed on her a nice sponge cake, she shouldn't walk away hungry.

When they got home, however, Gabby realized she had failed to write down the doctor's name. Then she forgot the conversation altogether.

Over the next few days Gabby found her granddaughter starting arguments over the smallest of provocations. One day the ostensible cause of the argument was the foul smell in the basement laundry room, where Jennifer was forced to do her own wash. The next day the cold weather and her lack of having the right clothes set her off. Gabby offered to go with her to buy new ones to supplement her wardrobe, insisting that they could use her dad's cash to bankroll the whole expedition. But Jennifer was not mollified.

And then Jennifer launched into the subject of going out alone. After two weeks of constant companionship she had begun to feel more like a conjoined twin than a granddaughter. Unsure of what to do with the request, and noting the agitation in Jennifer's voice, as if she were picking a fight, Gabby said she needed to think about it and went to the kitchen to ruminate over a cup of tea.

She knew right away that keeping Jennifer under lock and key was not the answer. Her home would appear less an oasis than a cell in which privileges would be extended but no autonomy. At the same time, Jennifer's brooding presence was stifling. Gabby could use a breather from this in her home.

But she had promised to be responsible, as Green had insisted, 24/7. Who knew what Jennifer would do?

Later that afternoon Gabby decided to give her approval. Jennifer would have her blessing to go out alone on the condition that she return at an agreed-upon hour and stay on the Upper West Side. Gabby, of course, managed to provide a healthy dose of guilt along with this concession. Gabby would be held responsible by the powers that be, and Jennifer knew who that was, back in L.A. Though it made her feel like a teen with a curfew, Jennifer quickly agreed to the terms if for no other reason than to get her nana off her back.

Of course, none of this stopped Gabby from playing private eye on Jennifer's first solo foray, tailing her granddaughter like some geriatric James Bond. More than a few eyebrows were raised as Gabby dramatically ducked behind cars and hid behind street vendors, her attention riveted on her granddaughter as Jennifer strolled east along 72nd Street. Her concentration was indeed so laser sharp that she failed to notice two cans of garbage blocking her path and took a rather noisy and nasty pratfall that sent rubbish tumbling in all directions. She shot up, wheezing, fighting in vain to see past a businessman who had rushed to her aid, catching a last glimpse of Jennifer as she slipped into the park and out of sight.

11

Entering the park off Central Park West and 72nd Street, Jennifer found a small pathway dotted by vendors hawking drinks and T-shirts, some emblazoned with the face of John Lennon and others heralding "Strawberry Fields." On one side of the pathway, an older man was playing Beatles songs on a boom box. On the other side, a young girl had a guitar and was entertaining a small group of people by singing about revolution and wanting to change the world. Moving down the path Jennifer immediately came upon a triangle-shaped parcel of land whose focus was a dazzling circular mosaic of inlaid stones. A nearby sign explained that the materials used in the artwork had been contributed by countries from around the world. In the center of the mosaic was one word in large letters: IMAGINE.

Jennifer paused for a few moments to read a marker describing how John Lennon and Yoko Ono had once enjoyed bringing their young son to this spot to play. It said

Lennon had been gunned down across the street in front of their apartment building, the Dakota. Jennifer noted the date of his assassination — December 8, 1980, the year she was born. She lifted her camcorder and filmed the word that dominated the mosaic. She focused on the gifts visitors had placed there: flowers, candles, a guitar pick, some incense sticks sending up a wispy tail of smoke, floating the aroma of magnolia on the air. And then her lens captured a disheveled mother and her young child sitting on a torn old sleeping bag on the grass nearby. She wondered if they had spent the night here. What was their life like? Where was the child's father? She decided she didn't want to think about it and abruptly turned away.

Jennifer continued to wend her way deeper into the park. She observed the life teeming all around her: in-line skaters speeding along the closed-off park streets; joggers pumping arms as they sprinted by; children being pushed on swings by moms, dads, and nannies; lovers sprawled out under trees. Even with all that was going on around her Jennifer was aware that she was very much alone. In fact, it struck her now that she hadn't truly been alone, out of the reach of others' observing eyes, since the night on the beach just before they found her. Pausing by a fountain with an angel that seemed to rise out of it, she took a deep breath, then exhaled forcefully. It was as if she were trying to clear the clutter from inside herself.

After walking for some time Jennifer climbed atop a large rock near the pathway. She closed her eyes and lay back, staring up through the sun-dappled leaves. It occurred to her that her nana had taken a pretty big risk letting her go off alone like this. True, Jennifer acknowledged to herself, there wasn't a whole lot Gabby could have done had Jennifer made her mind up to leave. But she had been willing to gamble that Jennifer wouldn't run, that she wouldn't immediately try to replicate the events of that night on the beach. That she could somehow be responsible. Why would her nana be willing to take a risk like that? she asked herself. The whole thing didn't make sense to her.

Jennifer pushed herself up on one arm and glanced around, the light dancing about her. It was beautiful here, she had to admit. She remembered walks she'd taken as a little girl with her mom and dad when they had visited her nana in New York. She must have been no more than five. She'd love to have been five again, an age when she didn't know anything much.

And then her eyes landed on a couple just below her on the rock. They were kissing passionately, their bodies pressed against each other as if they couldn't bear to be two people. Jennifer couldn't help but think of Phillip, the way his mouth felt on hers that first time and on so many nights thereafter. How they moved as one in their lovemaking and how she felt as if she were turning herself inside out, revealing all of herself to another for the first time. How afterward they would lie for hours in each other's arms, falling asleep curled up into the angles of each other's bodies. Jennifer wiped away the tears and quickly scrambled off the rock.

After taking a few steps Jennifer remembered her camcorder and climbed back up on the rock to retrieve it. The sound of a young woman giggling caused Jennifer to glance at the couple one more time. The young man was running his hand gently across his girlfriend's face, tickling her in the process. Jennifer's breath caught in her throat. *Don't trust him,* she thought in the young woman's direction. For some reason at that moment the couple suddenly noticed her. Embarrassed at being caught staring, Jennifer quickly hustled off the rock, running all the way out of the park back into the pounding blare of the city.

12

True to her word, Jennifer was back at the apartment an hour and a half later, to the appreciative nod of her much relieved nana. After that, Gabby didn't seem to mind Jennifer's going out alone. She was even pleasantly surprised when, while sharing tea and cinnamon rugelach with her one afternoon, Jennifer tossed out that her favorite walk was one that took her to the Belvedere Castle. Gabby knew well the fairy-tale edifice overlooking the Turtle Pond in the middle of Central Park.

Two days later Gabby was checking out the window of a nearby Barnes & Noble when she saw an announcement for a book signing that Wednesday evening at seven P.M. The book was entitled *Unleashing the Possibilities Within*, and the author was none other than the psychologist she now remembered Frieda touting — Larry Nevins, Ph.D. Gabby took it as a sign. If he was good enough for Frieda's nephew's son's cocaine addiction, not to mention Messieurs Barnes and Noble, then maybe he could work his magic with Jennifer.

Gabby called the psychologist's office that afternoon.

"Hello. My name is Gittel Zuckerman," she began enthusiastically, "and my good friend Frieda Steinberg gave the doctor her highest recommendation, which in her case is really some —"

"Who?" came the receptionist's curt response.

Gabby didn't follow. "Who *me* or who *her?*" she asked.

"What?"

"Maybe I wasn't clear. My name —"

"Yes, yes," the officious woman replied. "Now, who did you say recommended you to Dr. Larry's office?"

"Dr. *Larry?*" Gabby repeated in exaggerated fashion, finding the reference a tad too familiar for a therapist of any substance.

"Hello?"

"Yes, I'm here," Gabby caught herself. "I was saying that my dear friend Frieda Steinberg recommended —"

"Steinberg?"

"That's right."

"I don't know that name," the receptionist responded in a clipped, dismissive tone. "Is she a patient?"

89

"No. No. Her nephew . . ." Gabby started to explain and then immediately thought better of it. Apparently a person had to pass some kind of verbal test with the crazy lady making the appointments in order to actually get to see the mental health expert.

"Look, I have a granddaughter who needs a good therapist," Gabby blurted out with passion. "She has not been well. What am I saying, she took pills would choke a horse . . ." Gabby suddenly felt funny telling all this to a perfect stranger and stopped right there. "Let's just say, it wasn't good. We simply would like an appointment, preferably in the next few days." Gabby collected herself, waiting for a possible date.

There was a pause, then a businesslike reply. "Well, I'm afraid the doctor isn't really taking on any new patients right now."

"What? But we —"

"He has a very busy practice, I'm sure you understand. And now with his book . . ."

The woman couldn't have let me know this at the beginning of our nonconversation, Gabby muttered to herself. Not that it would have stopped her, she thought while regrouping. This killjoy on the other end of the phone was about to discover she was no match for the powerful obstinacy of Gabby Zuckerman. Gabby gathered herself up, creased her face with determination, and promptly launched into a spectacular outburst of shameless tears.

To her utter surprise she found the usually fail-safe tear routine did not budge this gorgon of a receptionist handling the therapist's appointments. That was it. Gabby pulled out her trump card. She insisted on speaking with Dr. Larry herself.

"I don't think that's going to be possible. I'm sorry, what did you say your name was?" came the condescending reply.

"My friends call me Gabby. You can call me Mrs. Zuckerman. And I suggest you tell the good doctor that my granddaughter's father is the *very* big, very hot, extremely *well-connected* Hollywood producer, Barry Stempler, who has but to make the call and Dr. Larry and his new book appear on *Oprah* like that!"

Not a minute later Dr. Larry himself was on the phone, enthusiastically booking Jennifer's appointment for the end of the week.

It had been difficult sharing Jennifer's story — the divorce, her mother's death, the suicide attempt — with the therapist over the phone. But she had promised Dr. Green she would follow through and she wanted to make good on that promise. That Friday,

Gabby insisted on going with Jennifer to the appointment — in part to offer moral support, but truth be told, more to ensure that Jennifer actually went to see the doctor.

"Why do I have to go to this guy?" Jennifer demanded angrily while Gabby was hailing a cab. "People just need to leave me alone."

"Maybe what you need is not so much for people to leave you alone, Jennifer, but to understand why you want so badly to *be* alone."

"Hey, there you go, just like a therapist, Nana. Everyone's a shrink these days," Jennifer shot back.

Jennifer seethed silently on the ride to the East Side. Later, as they rode in the elevator up to Dr. Larry's Park Avenue office, Gabby observed Jennifer nervously tapping her fingers on the wall, biting her lip in agitation.

Gabby was slightly amused when the receptionist proved to be effusively welcoming when they actually met face-to-face. After a few minutes Dr. Larry came out, introduced himself, and ushered Jennifer into his office. Gabby noticed her granddaughter's eyes flash, something she had never seen before. The look reminded her of an animal facing danger, like a horse about to be whipped, as if Jennifer were reentering a world in which she had been abused and to which she had now once more been condemned.

Gabby began to cough and had to hold on to the chair for dear life. With great difficulty she managed to get to the watercooler in the corner of the waiting room but found the cups had run out. She looked around for help, but the receptionist was busy on the phone. Cupping her hand, she scooped up a handful of water.

Leaning back against the wall, her breath still ragged, Gabby stared at the door through which her granddaughter had just disappeared. More than anything, she wished to be on the other side.

13

The moment she entered the room, Jennifer's heart began beating rapidly. Offered a choice of a couch swathed in dark leather or an aerodynamic recliner that appeared poised for space travel, Jennifer chose the former. She sat opposite Dr. Larry, who perched upright in his sleek winged-back leather chair, a self-contained mind jockey, notepad in hand, pen at the ready. Her attention was drawn to a thick gold bracelet on the psychologist's wrist, which jangled as he flipped his notepad to a new page. He likes to announce his authority, she noted, reversing the roles. She studied Dr. Larry closely. He had wavy, thinning salt-and-pepper hair that was neatly cropped; his slate-colored eyes were set off against a milk-white complexion apparently safely guarded from contact with sunlight. He was trim, almost wiry, with just a hint of a double chin. Holding up a finger, Dr. Larry scribbled now on his notepad. "Sorry," he said without looking up. "Just give me a moment."

Sure, Jennifer commented to herself, take all the time you want. Write a novel for all I care. There was a knock on the door and the receptionist poked her head in the room, apologizing for the intrusion. She needed a specific file if the session had not yet begun. Jennifer watched Dr. Larry magnanimously proffer the file from his desk and the receptionist sashay in. She caught a slight flirtation in the receptionist's giggle as the psychologist beckoned her close and whispered something in her ear, his index finger lingering against her hand as he passed over the requested item.

As Dr. Larry reluctantly returned his attention to his notepad, Jennifer noticed the wedding ring on his left hand. Immediately she conjured a scenario of afternoon trysts between the therapist and his receptionist. They probably took place right on the very couch where she was sitting! She shifted, staring down at the cushions, disgusted by the thought. Her father's face popped into her head. They're all alike, she told herself. Every one of them.

As the psychologist continued scribbling, Jennifer scanned the neatly appointed office. Large lithographs of pointillist art loomed on the walls, including one Jennifer recognized as *A Sunday Afternoon on the Is-*

land of La Grande Jatte. Her eye landed on the ornately framed diploma from Princeton University above the dark wooden desk. She became aware of the subdued lighting in the room, a characteristic she had long ago recognized as one of the tools therapists use to manufacture intimacy. Images from many past therapy sessions flooded Jennifer's mind. She had thought this particular mental merry-go-round was over for her. Hadn't she tried her best to close the door on it three weeks ago on Venice Beach? Now, against her will, she'd been drawn back, back to the pain that had driven her there in the first place, back to the center ring of this analytical circus. Jennifer felt her hands perspiring and her breathing growing ragged. Feelings she had frozen within suddenly threatened to thaw and pour out of her. She could feel the heat emanating from her flushed cheeks. She was angry at her nana for bringing her here and at herself for allowing it to happen.

"Now then, Jennifer," the therapist began, clearing his throat and nodding, "why don't you go right ahead and tell me a bit about yourself."

Jennifer shifted silently in her seat. It was bad enough she was in the room with this guy; she wasn't going to humor him by playing The Game. Dr. Larry allowed for the quiet in the room, giving her ample time to speak her mind. When she didn't offer a word he nodded again, tapping his pen once on the notepad.

"I can see that it's a little difficult for you to talk about yourself. Why don't we start by talking a bit about your childhood, your mother, father, any siblings? How does that sound?"

Why don't we start by knocking that stupid smile off your prissy face? How does that sound? Jennifer remained mute, staring blankly back at him in response.

She silently cursed her nana again for making her do this, her hands curling into fists. But as she watched Dr. Larry blather on, urging her to open up, she began to realize something. Had her nana not rescued her and brought her to New York, she'd have been forced to endure this crap on a daily basis. And with her father pulling the strings she'd have had no control over her life whatsoever.

". . . where you are emotionally. When your grandmother and I spoke briefly on the phone, she mentioned that you've been depressed. Could you tell me a little about that?" the psychologist prodded.

"I don't feel like it," Jennifer snapped back.

Dr. Larry emitted strained laughter. "You don't feel like it. Well, good, that's a beginning. Come on now, say more." And he leaned forward in his chair in anticipation.

"I don't think so." Jennifer spoke through gritted teeth and eyed the door.

"You don't think so?" The therapist nodded. "Well, we are having some difficulty today, aren't we?" Jennifer caught him glancing at the clock above the door.

"Let's talk about your grandmother," Dr. Larry offered impatiently. "Do you like your grandmother?"

Do I like my grandmother? How pathetic! Jennifer shook her head, glancing over at this lame therapist who probably cheated on his wife. He hadn't a clue how to approach her, she told herself. Staring back at the talking head in front of her she found herself suddenly thinking: *Who is this hotshot anyway? Just some suit with a gold trinket and an attitude.* And that thought lightened the heaviness within her. In fact, it made the whole experience seem downright amusing.

"Well, Dr. Larry — may I call you Dr. Larry?" she said, relishing his growing discomfort.

"Yes, of course. Everyone does," he responded evenly.

"You know that's just so darn cute," she said with a shake of her head. The therapist sat back rigidly in his chair, trying to read her.

"Dr. Larry," Jennifer continued, "I must have been to a zillion shrinks from the time my father cheated on my mom and me when I was a kid right up until three days before I tried to kill myself three weeks ago, and you know, Doctor, they have all been full of shit. Everyone asks how I feel about this and that. Hey, I swallowed half a bottle of Xanax. Doesn't that give you a fucking clue?"

Dr. Larry's face reddened. Pulling himself together, he moved to take back control of the session. "All right, Jennifer. Okay. Now you mentioned your father's cheating. You're clearly angry about that. Can you say more?"

Jennifer studied him a moment, silence weighing in the room.

"You got kids, Larry?"

The therapist drew himself up in his chair. "We're not here to discuss my family," he said evenly, though Jennifer noted the veins in his neck were doing the Macarena.

"Now, you see, right there, that's where you shrinks have it all wrong. You want access to our lives. You want to know about our *families* and our *feelings*. This is your job, okay, but did it ever occur to you geniuses with the fancy diplomas and jewelry that maybe, just maybe, the whole thing's just a little one-sided. Who wants to open up to someone who's a closed book? Got it?"

"What?" Dr. Larry blinked.

"You want to know about my family?" Jennifer enthused, enjoying playing by her own rules, "I want to know about yours. Now doesn't that seem logical?"

The therapist shook his bracelet and cleared his throat. "You want to know about my family?" he asked, shaking his head vigorously as if he might lose it right there.

"Yes, Doctor, I do," Jennifer said, waiting.

Dr. Larry pulled himself up straighter in his chair. "All right then, Jennifer. I'll play along. For a moment or two," he grinned, wrestling for composure.

Jennifer noticed the way he had started shifting in his seat. At the moment he opened his mouth to speak, she held a finger up in the air, putting him on hold. She asked for a piece of paper and a pen to take a few notes and thought Dr. Larry would go through the roof. Instead, holding himself on a tight leash, the psychologist handed over the requested items.

"Now, Doctor," Jennifer said sweetly, "why don't you start with your childhood. Mother? Father? Siblings?"

Dr. Larry pursed his lips, rubbing together the index finger and thumb on his left hand as if he might rub the skin off completely.

"What is it you would like to know?" he replied tersely, pulling at his crisp white collar.

"Your mother, she still living?"

"Yes, she's retired in Iowa."

"Now, as a child, did you like your mother, Dr. Larry?"

"How does my answering this question help you with your depression, Jennifer?" the therapist responded tersely.

"Never mind about that. Did you like your mother, Doctor?"

"All right, Jennifer, that's not relevant here," the psychologist muttered, his right foot tapping anxiously.

"Why not? Isn't that what all of you want to know, whether those of us who show up asking for your help got along with our parents when we were kids? Well, I'd like to know if the therapist who wants to get inside my head felt affection for his own mother as a child. Is that such a stretch?"

Dr. Larry had become so puffed with

outrage and his lips so firmly sealed, Jennifer thought he might actually achieve liftoff.

"You see, I have this theory, Doc." Jennifer leaned forward from her perch on the sofa. "I say that more often than not people who become shrinks come from some of the most repressed segments of our population. They figure they can work their neuroses out through the rest of us and get paid for it. In fact, hear me out on this: Some have made an entire career recycling the same six words over and over again — HOW DOES THAT MAKE YOU FEEL?!"

In the waiting room, Gabby was wading through a large-print *Reader's Digest* when the door to Dr. Larry's office flew open and the apoplectic therapist ushered a beaming Jennifer from his office. "I'm sorry," he whispered hoarsely to Gabby. She stared at the noticeable tic he had developed.

As he disappeared behind his door, an energized Jennifer shouted, "*You're* sorry? Think about your mother!" Turning to the receptionist she whispered in mock confidence, "I realize the only reason they call him a shrink is because, you know, he has a hard time finding his own dick. You tell him not to worry too much about it!"

Jennifer glanced over at Gabby, whose chin had dropped in shock.

"You all right, Nana? You look a little pale."

Gabby stared back, wondering what this grinning stranger had done with her depressed granddaughter.

"I'm a little hungry. You hungry, Nana?" Jennifer asked casually as she paced.

Gabby lifted her eyebrows, thunderstruck. "I . . . could eat," she heard herself say over her confusion.

As they left the office, Gabby glanced back at the stunned face of the receptionist and gave the woman a sweet little smile.

"My granddaughter," she whispered. "She likes a good . . . discussion. You have a nice day."

14

"The man had a meltdown like you wouldn't believe. He was like Homer Simpson with PMS. It was freaky!" Jennifer pronounced, shaking her head and grinning.

Over turkey sandwiches and cream soda Jennifer related to a flustered Nana the highlights of her encounter with the highly touted Dr. Larry.

"You gotta know he's banging that receptionist," she pronounced with relish between bites.

"Jennifer!" Gabby gasped, her eyes blinking at the language and then yet again as the image registered.

"Oh, please. You saw the way he leaned over her when he came out to get me. Any closer, he'd have needed a condom." Jennifer hiccuped, laughing at her own joke as she guzzled the cream soda with a thirst Gabby hadn't seen before.

Gabby listened to her unwind. She nodded, smiling weakly at Jennifer's colorful references. But inside she was worried.

Not only about Jennifer's dramatic change in mood at the therapist's office, but by the fact that Dr. Larry seemed unable to help her. What would this mean for Jennifer's future mental health? she wondered. If the top shrink in New York couldn't handle this girl, how could Gabby? She thought of phoning Dr. Green and reporting the failure.

And yet, despite her deep concerns about the implications of this fiasco, Gabby couldn't help but be struck by something new emanating from her granddaughter. It was the glimmer of a smile and the effortless laughter coming from Jennifer. Gabby also had a long-standing mistrust of the health profession. As far as she was concerned, people were far too ready to give control over their own bodies to perfect strangers. Gabby realized that this rejection of Dr. Larry might be okay — in fact, possibly very good. It had helped Jennifer feel her own strength, regain her voice. Gabby relaxed a bit more and, eyes dancing, recalled Jennifer's proclamation about the size of Dr. Larry's private parts.

"What made you say such a thing about his — you know?"

"Don't know. It just popped into my head," Jennifer replied, grinning.

"Well, the man must have bathed in aftershave. And as I always say, never trust a man who wears too much cologne," Gabby observed, breaking into a giggle even Jennifer couldn't resist.

As they strolled along Columbus Avenue, Jennifer grew more subdued. She did not, however, pull away when Gabby slipped a hand under her arm as the two walked back to the apartment. Jennifer seemed lost in her own thoughts. Gabby worried about how to proceed with her end of the bargain: How could she keep Jennifer until Thanksgiving now?

Gabby knew that Jennifer would never consent to an appointment with another therapist, at least not at this stage of recovery. If Green insisted Jennifer go, Gabby could see her cutting a swath through the jungle of the New York mental health community, decimating an entire profession. But failure to have a local therapist sign off on Jennifer was tantamount to sending her away. Gabby envisioned white-coated orderlies jumping out of the bushes in the park, kidnapping Jennifer and returning her to California. There her father would most assuredly have her declared incompetent and would hand her over to some psychiatric facility where people wouldn't care whose granddaughter she was. No, she was

Jennifer's only advocate, Gabby told herself. She would have to think of something.

As twilight fell, they arrived back at the apartment, chilled by the October air, exhausted yet satisfied. Gabby immediately set about steeping some peppermint tea while Jennifer changed into her gray oversize sweats. She next arranged some kindling atop crumpled pages from the day's *New York Times,* added a couple of small logs, and lit a fire in the fireplace. Donning a cotton robe, Gabby slipped into her poofy rabbit-shaped slippers and joined Jennifer in the living room on the braided rug in front of the fireplace. Gabby handed her a mug of hot tea and cozied up against the sofa.

They sat and sipped at their tea for the better part of an hour, their silence punctuated now and again by the sparks popping from a log. Gabby watched as the flames played in reflection across Jennifer's face. In her mind, at least for this one night, her granddaughter seemed to have called a truce with her demons.

But Gabby worried about tomorrow, asking herself: How long would this improvement last? Was this a sign Jennifer had turned any kind of corner? How could Gabby placate Jennifer's father, not to mention Dr. Green, long enough to give her a chance to find her way? And of greatest consequence, why wasn't Lili here when Jennifer needed her the most? What kind of God, Gabby wondered, takes a young vibrant mother and leaves an aging, unhealthy grandmother in her place?

For her part, Jennifer was recalling the long line of therapists she had known. There had been Miss What Color Are Your Feelings after her parents' divorce. Mr. Give Yourself a New Tape after finding her mother in tears so often Jennifer had refused to see her father for several months, and Dr. Happy to Prescribe, into whose office Barry had ushered her less than twenty-four hours after her mom's funeral.

Those first two therapists weren't all that bad, not really, Jennifer told herself. They had been nurturing, compassionate. It was just that Jennifer had rebelled at having to be there at all. Therapy was one more reminder of the pain that forced her into the therapist's office to begin with, a hurt that fostered resentment. As for Dr. Happy, Jennifer found his approach toward symptoms of depression, with its accompanying loss of purpose and motivation, could best be expressed in the motto: "To feel great, medicate." And for two of her college years she had been the willing recipient of Dr. Happy's method of elation through sedation, keeping her pain at arm's length and reality even farther away. Discovering a world beyond her prescriptions, Jennifer eventually phased out Dr. Happy's services in favor of a veritable grab bag of alternative drugs — coke, Ecstasy, and PCP arriving in something known as the peace pill.

Her thoughts turned to Phillip, the one person Dr. Larry had not thought to ask her about. For a full year Jennifer had assumed she might be free of all therapists. Until she met Phillip Coskey, a candidate for a Ph.D. in English literature and the man destined, in her opinion, to be the love of her life. Here finally was the man who would rid her of her pervasive sadness, going back to her parents' divorce and the loss of the mother she had loved and counted on more than anyone else. Phillip had been the white knight of her childhood fairy tales, the prince she had long dreamed would rescue her from a life she had no wish to live. He alone could fill the void within her, the feeling that she would never be good enough, pretty enough, worthy enough. His love would at long last banish the darkness in which she felt trapped.

They met in her senior year when he was

beginning his graduate studies at Santa Barbara. Jennifer was drawn to his passion from the start, the way he drank deeply from life, embracing every moment. Phillip made no apologies for his boldness or the wealth of his feelings. She adored his reading aloud from Byron and thrilled to his public displays of love, including his ritual of greeting her with a bunch of wildflowers when they met at the café on campus twice a week. At home he could excitedly discuss Shelley while giving her a massage. Invariably, they would end up making love as if the two of them alone were responsible for the continued existence of the world. Most of all, Phillip seemed nothing like her father. Jennifer was certain her mom would have approved.

It had all seemed so perfect to her and she had desperately wanted to believe such perfection existed. At least that's what she told the all-too-hip feminist analyst — Ms. Men Hate Their Mothers, So They Dump Us — who had been the last of the Jennifer Stempler cycle of therapists until today's encounter with Dr. Larry.

Ten months into their relationship, Jennifer had moved into Phillip's condo. She had been sleeping there for months anyway and it seemed to both of them a logical progression. They had begun talking openly of the future, making plans for marriage, dreaming of where they would honeymoon, speaking of a family, the places they would travel, the dreams they would fulfill together. Three months into the new arrangement, she came home to find that Phillip had made her a beautiful meal of pasta marinara and a lovely salad. He had even opened a bottle of Chianti to go with it. Jennifer wasn't altogether surprised because he had always done something like this on the monthly anniversary of the day they had first met. It had been their special tradition. Usually there would be a flower waiting for her by her plate — a bird-of-paradise, a delphinium, sometimes simply a sweet yellow daffodil. His thoughtfulness was one of the reasons she loved him so much, and why she knew that her life could be better than her dreams.

Before they could enjoy their meal, however, Jennifer noticed that Phillip seemed agitated, on edge. She wondered if perhaps his courseload was weighing on him. She offered to type a paper of his that was due so he could concentrate on his thesis. That act of kindness was apparently too much for Phillip. He confessed that he just wasn't ready to make such a big commitment.

"Do you want to change your thesis topic?" she asked him, confused.

He coughed and finally said that he simply couldn't go through with their marriage plans. "Of course I love you," he said. "You will always be the love of my life." And then he asked her to move out.

Jennifer just couldn't wrap her mind around the suddenness of it all. Devastated beyond reason, Jennifer tormented herself with the question: Why does every man I care about in my life leave me? First it had been her father, whose love she had to admit she yearned for, and then Phillip, the man who had made her believe she could open her heart and trust again. She had been suckered, she told herself, into buying a fairy tale. From deep within her came the voice of utter condemnation: They left because something is so wrong with you it cannot be fixed.

"A penny for your thoughts," Gabby said softly, returning her granddaughter to the present.

Jennifer hesitated, letting out a long, slow breath. Then, feeling there was nothing to lose, she shared with her nana all of the history she'd been turning over in her mind. Slowly, and with details she'd long repressed, Jennifer brought Gabby into the world of loss, betrayal, prescription drugs, and therapists that had been her universe for so long. She had never found a way of escaping it all. That is, until she looked at all the doors closed in her life and decided to take a final exit. In the end, even that door had been slammed shut.

"But why was it I didn't know all this?" Gabby insisted, her voice laced with sadness and confusion.

"Mom always felt you had lived through your own hell, Nana. It was always easier to let you believe everything was all right with me. Besides, as far as I was concerned you were still busy mourning her. I mean, she was your only daughter. I couldn't add my crap to your life. And even if I wanted to, I figured you didn't really know about things like this."

"You say you wanted me to believe everything was all right," Gabby responded. "But the divorce, it was not all right. And your mother being taken from us so senselessly, that was *definitely* not all right."

"No. But after she was gone, I remembered how much she had wanted to protect you. Can you understand that, Nana?" Jennifer said, turning away, exhausted and sorry she had brought it up at all.

"And by trying this suicide, this way you

were sparing me heartache, meydele?" Gabby replied firmly, never taking her eyes off her granddaughter.

Jennifer faced her squarely, working to keep a lid on her emotions. "By the time I'd made that decision, you weren't in the picture anymore. I know it will sound selfish, Nana, but all I could see was me. And that, I'm here to tell you, was not a sight I cared for very much."

Gabby's voice suddenly rose with indignation. "How can you say such words? Today you were a Joan of Arc, an Emma Lazarus, refusing to bow to the tyranny of one more therapist! You were a thing of beauty. You let the world know you would not be pushed around!"

Jennifer smiled sadly at her nana's fierceness and her overblown depiction of her actions. "It was a stunt, what I did today, Nana. It didn't take courage or eloquence or any particular insight. It was just my way of saying to the therapists of the world that they mean nothing to me. There is nothing they can tell me about myself I don't already know and in far greater detail. You see, Nana, the thing of it is, contrary to what people may think, suicide is not an act of confusion but of clarity."

Jennifer propped herself up on her knees

and turned around to face Gabby. Even in the darkness, Jennifer could make out the expression of bewilderment in Gabby's eyes. And the profound hurt there as well.

Jennifer shook her head, not wanting to add to her nana's anguish. "I'll get us some hot tea," she said, leaving Gabby staring intently into the fire as if miraculously she might find the answers there that eluded her.

When Jennifer returned with more tea, Gabby warmed her hands around the base of one of the mugs, trying to calm herself. She waited for Jennifer to sit down once again and then asked the question she most feared asking.

"Jennifer, are you saying that even now, with the way you asserted yourself today, you would wish for your life to be over?"

The silence that followed her question filled Gabby with a dread so heavy it threatened to sink her heart. Jennifer continued to sip, her attention focused on a small birch log that had fallen from its perch atop the fire and was burning now off to the side. At long last, she spoke.

"Oh," she said, her voice trailing away like smoke. "I don't know."

For a moment, Gabby sat there in horror, as if a window she needed to remain open was being nailed shut and she was helpless to stop the action. She wept softly, lost in the sadness of Jennifer's admission.

At the sound of her weeping, Jennifer had pulled herself up onto the sofa, placing a hand on her nana's shoulders, stroking her gently.

"None of this is your fault, Nana, none of it. I don't mean for you to be hurt, you have to know that. Maybe I shouldn't have come. You know? It just makes it all harder for you, for me."

Gabby wiped her eyes, coughing long and hard. The pain in her chest now had nothing to do with emphysema and it would not go away. Jennifer pulled a box of tissues near her grandmother and retrieved a glass of water. When Gabby could once again swallow, she blew her nose hard, her face suddenly blank.

"It's not supposed to be like this," she said softly. "A woman is not supposed to bury her own daughter." She hesitated, as if barely believing such a thing could ever be. "But, meydele" — she trembled — "a granddaughter?" And now her tears fell with abandon, a river without end.

"It will be all right," Jennifer said.

And after she had worn herself out with crying and ragged coughing, Gabby mercifully fell asleep where she lay on the sofa.

116

Jennifer covered her with a large afghan, kissed her twice upon the forehead, and then quietly, taking her camcorder, slipped out into the New York night.

15

In the park Jennifer watched an elderly couple walking hand in hand under the street lamp. The gentleman wore a long gray coat and an old-fashioned fedora. The woman was in a full-length dress that looked to be about as ancient as she was, with a white woolen cape drawn about her. As they strolled arm in arm Jennifer thought she would tape them. She fiddled with the camera case she had brought and then thought, *What's the point?* The gentleman paused to blow on the woman's hands, rubbing them vigorously in his to warm them. He then kissed the back of each hand. They smiled at each other and walked on.

Jennifer allowed herself a sad smile that vanished quickly.

She walked for some time before finding the spot she had chosen and sat down on the glacier rock overlooking a small pond below. Jennifer caught sight of the stars reflected back at her on the surface of the water. She sat for a while, staring up at the night sky.

She then pulled the camera out and trained it on the small points of light but found the machine was too weak to pick them out.

Reaching into the pocket of her coat, Jennifer pulled out a brown vial, laying it on her lap. She slipped a small bottle of water out of her other pocket and took a long swig. She picked up the vial, studied it, then glanced up at the stars.

"I can't do this anymore, you know?" she whispered to the recorder that was still running. "I'm sorry. Forgive me. 'Night, Mom. Love you. You, too, Nana."

She lifted the camcorder one more time and tried again to focus it on the star-studded heavens. She could make out only blurry lights. She put the camera down and took in the heavens with her naked eye. With no warning, a shooting star arced across the darkness, causing Jennifer to gasp in surprise. She followed its trail before the brilliant light flamed out and faded into the cold October night.

16

Gabby awoke with a dull headache. She looked around to get her bearings, realized she hadn't fallen asleep in her own bed, and sadly remembered the events of the night before. Noticing the afghan tucked around her, she was touched. Jennifer hadn't wanted to disturb her and had evidently retired to Gabby's bedroom for the night.

Getting to her feet, she noticed the time on the clock above the mahogany side table. A quarter to eight in the morning — for someone used to rising with the dawn, this was truly sleeping in. Putting on her slippers, she shuffled through the hall to the kitchen, put on the coffee, then made her way to her bedroom to check if Jennifer might be ready for her morning cup. Finding the bed undisturbed, its odd-shaped pillows where she always put them, she froze. Jennifer might have gotten up early and made the bed in the exact same fashion as she always did, but something told Gabby otherwise. Alarmed, she called out Jennifer's name. As she feared, there was no answer.

Panicking, Gabby rushed to the front hallway, awkwardly slipping on the throw rug in her desperation. Reaching out to steady herself against the wall, she began coughing, gasping for breath. And then she saw it, propped up there against the front door — a small white envelope with her name on it. Gabby's heart was racing with fear as she nervously fumbled with the unsealed envelope, pulling from it a note on yellow-lined paper. It read simply: "I love you, Nana. Now and for always." And it was signed, "Your meydele."

Gabby's head felt as if it would explode. She screamed, "No, no, NO! Don't, my little one, please!"

As she quickly changed into pants and a pullover, her breathing grew labored and raspy. Donning the first footwear she got her hands on, a pair of floppy black rain boots, she snatched a ski cap and a heavy wool coat from the closet and burst out the door. As she hurried down the stairs, gasping, pounding the railing impatiently, she realized she hadn't the slightest idea where to go. She knew only that she must find Jennifer and stop her before it was too late, before she lost her granddaughter forever.

Emerging into the cold day, she called for Jennifer several times, looking fearfully up and down the block. She closed her eyes to shut out the terror engulfing her. Think, Gabby, she told herself. Where would she go? Where, where? She knew of only one place.

Gabby ran as fast as her frail legs would carry her, narrowly avoiding bumping into two nannies pushing infants in their carriages. She didn't wait for the walk signal at 72nd Street, leaving a slew of honking cars in her wake. And then, wheezing badly, she was in the park. About to pass out, she paused at a bench, hanging on to it, overcome by coughing.

A jogger passed nearby and, overhearing the commotion, made a detour. "Can I help you?" he asked, leaning over her solicitously. Still puffing, Gabby looked up in confusion. The young man's eyes were deep blue. Dressed in an NYU sweatshirt, purple running shorts, and a Yankees cap, he appeared to be in his mid-twenties. Strong and healthy, she thought. She squinted and swallowed hard, gasping for breath, studying his solid build, the sweat pouring off his body. And just like that, she was struck with inspiration. Startling the jogger with her sudden fierceness, Gabby barked out an order worthy of a wounded commander in chief.

"My granddaughter," she said imperiously, puffing and wheezing. "No time. Bend down now, please!"

Somewhat bewildered, the runner hesitated. Perhaps she had Alzheimer's? Or she was lost?

"There's no time. Do it now!" Gabby demanded, and this time, out of an instinct for self-preservation, the young man kneeled down. To his utter amazement, Gabby clambered onto his back like a jockey atop a racehorse. Perched aloft her newly acquired younger legs, she cried out in an invigorated voice: "To the castle! Shake the leg God gave you and giddyup!"

17

The bewildered young man bore his wheezing burden as best he could in the direction of Belvedere Castle. Carefully picking his way down a set of stairs at the fountain of the Angel of Bethesda, he arduously galloped up the hill by the Central Park boathouse and hurtled down a pathway lined with flaming maple and silver poplar. Along the way he wondered who the hell the madwoman on his back was, her cough in his ears, her rain boots digging into his ribs. This whole thing was positively insane, he told himself. His lungs were on fire, his sides ached, and he was going to miss the mandatory morning lecture. And yet something about Gabby's determination told him the danger she spoke of was all too real.

Struggling to cover ground, the bedraggled fellow managed to gasp out tidbits about himself in an attempt to normalize the situation. "Name's Charlie . . . Charlie Sosne . . . from Vermont . . . law student at NYU." Gabby gripped his neck tightly so as not to fall off, nearly strangling him in the process. Charlie came to understand from the information she breathed into his ear that her troubled granddaughter was depressed and in danger of taking her life, that this mission they were on was a desperate gamble.

"You remind me of my grandmother," he shouted back. "Died last year. She was" — suddenly heading down a short hill, his voice bouncing with every step — "a fight-er like you."

As they paused for traffic winding through the park, Charlie gasped for air, sweat streaming down his face. Gabby did her best to blot up the sweat with her sleeve as they jolted forward across the road. Suddenly Charlie's foot caught on the curb, sending them lurching forward. Miraculously, he regained his legs. The castle appeared up ahead.

Close to exhausted, Charlie carried Gabby up the promontory of Vista Rock. Gabby scanned the landscape ahead. There was no sign of Jennifer. Could her hunch have been wrong?

As they reached the castle grounds Charlie slowed, his breathing ragged. Gabby tapped him on the shoulder and slid to the ground. Her body was weak from exertion, but she pushed forward. "Come with me," she said, moving as quickly as her flagging legs could carry her.

The two ran side by side down one open-air corridor and around a group of Japanese tourists, Gabby's heart pounding with fear. Charlie found himself caught up in the mission into which he'd been drafted, wanting to find the mystery woman, praying desperately that this Don Quixote of a grandmother would find her search rewarded.

Turning a corner along the promenade by the castle wall, Gabby stopped suddenly, Charlie in her wake nearly bumping into her. There before them, sitting atop the stone railing overlooking Turtle Pond, sat Jennifer. For a moment, Gabby stood transfixed at the sight of her granddaughter. Charlie, too, could not take his eyes off the delicate young woman poised above the water's edge. Then, as if sensing their presence, Jennifer slowly looked up.

"Nana?" she uttered in disbelief. "Who . . ." She looked at the sweaty young man by Gabby's side, confused.

Gabby approached Jennifer, trembling, unsure of what to say.

"I thought I might not see you again, meydele. I didn't know where . . ." Her voice faltered as she searched for the right words.

"I had to find you and . . . this nice young man, like a horse he carried me. But you're here, you didn't . . ." She broke off, her hands muffling her cry.

"No," Jennifer said softly, drained of emotion, "I wanted to, but . . . I kept seeing your face, Nana."

She looked directly into her grandmother's eyes. "But this place, how did you know?" Jennifer asked, seeking to make sense of it all.

"Nana's job is to know, darling," Gabby whispered.

Not ten feet away, the tired young jogger watched in silence, moved and full of questions himself.

Gabby took Jennifer by the hand and, beckoning to Charlie to follow, led her dazed granddaughter out of the park.

18

Charlie escorted the women over to Columbus Avenue, where he was going to catch the subway to the Village. But Gabby felt more than grateful to her trusty steed and insisted he come to her apartment for a home-cooked meal. Gracefully, he took a rain check and they exchanged numbers. "I don't usually share that information on my first 'gait,' " he quipped, "but in your case I'll make an exception." Well, a sense of humor isn't everything, Gabby thought, smiling doubtfully. Giving her a bear hug, Charlie smiled warmly and whispered in her ear, "I'm happy for you."

He turned next to say good-bye to Jennifer, and as he did, his manner caught Gabby's attention. It was the way he took her granddaughter's hand between both of his, very old-country and intimate, as if he knew her or thought he should. For his part, when Charlie looked into Jennifer's eyes, something familiar there held him. He smiled and said, "You've got a great nana there. You take care of her." Then, with a playful neigh, he galloped over toward Broadway and vanished into the crowd.

Gabby and Jennifer headed toward the apartment, famished and worn out. The effects of the morning's crisis on Gabby were now making themselves felt. Acute pain worked its way through her overtaxed lungs. As the two crossed 72nd Street at Columbus, Gabby hacked and wheezed in a particularly violent fashion. Jennifer braced her nana, trying vainly to flag down a cab. Gabby, however, insisted on continuing across the street, where, with Jennifer's help, she held on to a lamppost until the coughing subsided.

"Let's take a break, Nana. A little food, all right?" Jennifer said, leading her into a modest diner on the other side of Columbus.

The restaurant might not have been much to look at, but at that moment it was an oasis. Settled into a booth, some hot tea and toast in her, Gabby soon felt immeasurably restored. She sat back, the twinkle in her eyes returning, enjoying the sight of her granddaughter hungrily downing a stack of pancakes she'd soaked in maple syrup.

"I needed a little something, you were right. It's a m'chayah."

"What's that?" Jennifer asked through a mouthful of pancake.

"M'chayah? I guess you'd call it anything that makes you feel yourself again. Like hot tea on a cold day. Holding a baby's hand. A little something that makes you feel alive."

"Umm." Jennifer nodded, taking a gulp of coffee as she signaled the waitress for more. She assured a skeptical Gabby that the caffeine would have absolutely no effect on her ability to get some much-needed rest. "At this point I could fall asleep in Times Square!"

For the first time that morning, Gabby breathed deeply and without incident. Only now could she take stock of the crisis they had both just endured. Her granddaughter could have taken her life. Or at the very least, run away. But she had chosen to do neither. That was a hopeful sign, Gabby told herself, and she would cling to it with every fiber of her being.

She remembered the call she owed Dr. Green. Barry Stempler would have her head for that. He'd been leaving messages and she wasn't sure she could get away with simply ignoring them any longer. But at the same time Gabby was convinced that Jennifer's having chosen not to end her life the night before was proof she was on the edge of a breakthrough. Rushing her out to a therapist, any therapist, after the events of that morning would be devastating. Jennifer would surely see this as a betrayal, and worse, could use it as an excuse to run away. Jennifer was fragile, that was abundantly clear. No, Gabby decided, if Jennifer had to have a therapist, it was going to be her grandmother. Convincing Jennifer's father of that, however, would be another story. Gabby felt the sudden need for schnapps, but the diner didn't serve liquor.

After one last cup of coffee and a few bites of a bagel, Jennifer was definitely finished. Gabby, delighted at Jennifer's appetite, joked that there was more food at her apartment, just in case. Rejuvenated and ready for bed, the two decided they could make the last three blocks on foot, Gabby insisting the crispness of the air would help. October was over. It was the first day of a new month, she realized. November — what a time for a new beginning.

As they walked, Gabby impishly brought up the subject of Charlie. What were Jennifer's impressions? Had she noticed the way he held her hand?

"Oh, please, Nana, give the love-doctor thing a rest. The first thing this guy hears about me is I'm preparing to off myself!" Jennifer quipped.

"It was the truth," Gabby remarked, wondering what that had to do with being attracted to a person.

"Yes, Nana," Jennifer cracked, "but that information, no offense, is sort of a downer, you know? I don't think dating is an option here. A guy hears a girl's suicidal and he's probably not thinking, Hey, this one is different, I'm taking her home to the folks."

Gabby failed to see the humor, insisting Charlie was a good-looking young man. A law student at that. What wasn't to like? Most important, he had a good heart. Jennifer shouldn't be so quick to dismiss the possibility of their connecting simply because of how they'd met.

"Now you want to talk strange first meetings, take my Itzik and me . . ."

Jennifer dismissed the whole topic out of hand with a wry grin. "Come on. No offense, Nana, but only a hopeless romantic would try to play matchmaker to a screwed-up girl like me."

Gabby studied her as they paused for a light. "Someday soon, Jennifer, you will discover you are worthy of love."

Gabby had spoken with such confidence

in the certainty of this outcome that Jennifer was temporarily silenced. They walked on without another word. And then they were back at the apartment building, thankful to be heading up to the promise of hot baths and soft pillows.

Inserting the key in the lock, Gabby paused, turning to Jennifer, reaching up and touching her cheek tenderly. "I'm glad you're here with me, meydele."

Pushing open the apartment door, Gabby stepped into the vestibule and froze.

"I hope you don't mind?" came the deep voice. "I explained to the landlord my daughter was here and gave him a little something to let me in."

Jennifer pushed by her nana and was shocked to see her father emerging from the shadows of the hallway.

"Dad!"

"Hello, Jennifer. Are you all right?" he asked, his concern mixed with anger as his gaze flicked back to Gabby.

"Yes, but why are you here?"

"Ask your nana about that," Barry said, his eyes flashing in Gabby's direction. "We had a deal, one it seems she was unable or unwilling to keep."

"I was going to call you back, Barry," Gabby offered, clearing her throat.

"Yes, well, a person would do well not to count on what you were *going* to do."

"Don't talk to her like that," Jennifer demanded, taking a step toward him in anger. "And I'm not some film project you can wheel and deal. I won't be dealt, you hear me?"

"Jennifer, stay out of this now. This is between your nana and me," Barry cautioned.

"This is about my life. Don't talk about it as if I'm not here," Jennifer shouted.

"Jennifer, listen to me," he tried to reason, moving forward. They could now see Jennifer's travel bag on the floor behind him.

"What are you doing with my things?"

"Look, I took the red-eye because your nana here hasn't gotten you the psychological help she'd promised she would. Dr. Green let me know he has received no reports from any shrink to date. I show up at your apartment, no one's around, doors wide open. Anyone could have been waiting for you here. That doesn't exactly make me feel you're safe. Now, I've packed those things of yours I could find . . ."

"Barry, listen to me," Gabby insisted.

"I'm not going anywhere. Not with you!" Jennifer interjected.

Barry took a step toward her. "Listen, Jen.

I know I screwed up big-time with you. But I want to make it up to you."

"Oh, you do." Jennifer smiled mockingly. "*Now* you want to play daddy? You weren't there for Mom or me. I did my best to take care of her, you know, but you're the reason she was so sad all the time. I've always known it. And you're the reason she was on foot that day the drunk driver ended her life. I'll never forgive you for that."

"Jennifer, let your father and me —" Gabby softly cut in, but Jennifer was having none of it.

"No, Nana, this is about me, my life!" She turned back to Barry. "What gives you the right to come in here and think you can tell me what I'm going to do with it? If I want to live, I live. You got that? I want to die, that's my goddamn choice!"

"I'm your father, damn it!" Barry shouted above her.

Jennifer nodded with contempt. "Yeah, that's right, you donated your sperm and wrote a few checks."

"That's unfair, Jen, and you know it."

"Gimme a break. Go back to your pretty little wife and baby and play daddy for them, okay?"

Gabby stood off to the side as Jennifer leaned her back against the wall, squeezing her eyes shut as if she could make her father disappear.

Barry appeared to be fighting to calm himself, wrestling with the words he wanted to say. "Listen, Jen. I know it probably hurts that I'm married again, have a little girl. Like I've tossed you and your mother out . . ." There was silence. "I'm sorry to say this in front of your nana. She's a good woman, really. And your mother, she was a good woman. The best. I didn't know how to deserve her."

"Don't," Jennifer said, anguishing over these words.

"I've grown up, I think . . . and with Cynthia, I feel like I've finally learned how to give love. With Briana, it's like I've woken up from some kind of . . . I was in the delivery room when she was born, Jen, it was amazing seeing her coming into the world, and suddenly I realized . . . I'd missed having that with you." Barry moved closer. Jennifer blocked him with her palm, keeping him at a distance.

"I know I've given you pain," Barry said, lips quivering, "and God knows, you hate me. But there are things I want to say to you, share with you, things I couldn't share before."

Jennifer looked up at him, his eyes

pleading. Her mind raced back to all the times in her life when she yearned for him to hold her, to tell her he loved her. At one time, simple words and actions would have meant the world. If only he had showed up at all her birthday parties, the school plays she took part in, instead of running around doing whatever it was he did that was so all-important. She had been desperate for his words of approval, thirsty to have him tell her, just once, that he was proud of her. For what seemed like an eternity, no one said a word.

Barry studied his daughter's crossed arms, the look of defiance. "Isn't there some kind of statute of limitations on hating your father?" he asked gently.

Jennifer stared back at him. "I don't know, Dad. If there is, I haven't found it yet."

"Listen, Barry," Gabby piped up, trying to shift the confrontation back to the immediate source of contention, "Jennifer's remaining in New York. I've been avoiding calling Dr. Green because the truth is, conventional therapy isn't going to work with Jennifer."

Barry exhaled sharply in frustration. "You've got some degree I don't know about?"

"She's my nana," Jennifer responded

without raising her voice. "Try speaking to her with just a little respect."

"How about speaking to your father . . ." he tossed back, but Gabby cut him off before things could escalate yet again.

"We tried one therapist, highly recommended. It was a disaster."

"You listen to me, Gabby. She's my daughter, and she's coming home with me!"

"In your dreams!" Jennifer barked.

Losing control, Barry pointed his finger at Gabby. "Look, this isn't just me, it's the doctors. Now, why don't you just be quiet for once and let —"

"She is the flesh of *my* daughter, and I will not be silent!" Gabby said, her voice rising, startling both Barry and Jennifer alike.

Gabby continued, emotions still running high. "With every fiber that lives in my body I believe Jennifer is getting better. I can't explain it all, but I swear it on the memory of my daughter."

"Don't go throwing Lili into this," Barry muttered impatiently.

"Lili *is* a part of this!" Gabby fired back. "This is her daughter, too, and I am the one who speaks for her today. This is not some movie set where you can throw your weight around and everyone agrees with the great producer. This is life, Barry, your daughter's life. She deserves better. She deserves love. You can threaten me any way you like, but I am telling you one thing — Jennifer goes home with you now over my dead body." And with that, Gabby planted herself in the doorway with conviction.

There was a pause. Barry stood, breathing hard, tie askew, looking from one to the other.

Taking a step toward Jennifer, he tried to reason with her. "I want what's best for you, Jen, you have to believe that," he pleaded.

Jennifer stared at him with cold detachment. "*Now* you want a relationship with me? *Now* you know what it means to love someone? What about all those years you weren't there for me? What about your marriage to Mom? Does that mean you never loved her, not even in the beginning? That you never loved *us?* I've appreciated the money, paying the rent and all. That was nice, thanks. As for the rest . . . it's just a little too late now, you know?"

Barry looked over at Gabby as if she held all the power, his eyes filled with hurt. "Well, Gabby, I guess you win."

"This is not about me winning or you losing," Gabby quietly said. "It's about Jennifer."

"I need to know that she'll be back in Los

Angeles by Thanksgiving as promised, Gabby. The people who know tell me I've taken a huge risk letting you run things. I don't know. But we can't risk not getting her help if whatever it is you're doing doesn't work. Are we still on the same page here? Please tell me we are." For the first time, Barry appeared broken, searching for Gabby's strength.

She nodded, smiling gently. "I promise you she will be there. And if I fail to keep my word, then by all means, feel free to do what you have to do."

"Nana?" Jennifer erupted, hurt, her eyes questioning.

"Barry, she is going to be all right," Gabby assured him, as if convincing herself as well. "She *has* to be." The two looked at each other, wanting to believe it, yet each still not quite trusting the other.

Barry turned back to Jennifer. "Jen, I'll see you in twenty-four days. I will be waiting for you."

He bent forward to try to kiss her on the head and she drew back. Barry crossed glumly to the door and Gabby stepped aside to let him by, the two eyeing each other intently. Then, looking back at his daughter, Barry paused, adding almost wistfully, "I know it may not be something you want to hear, Jen, but there's a little girl back in L.A. who'd like to get to know her sister." Then he turned and slipped out the door.

Gabby and Jennifer held their breath a minute, half expecting him to come back.

"He doesn't have armed guards out there waiting to haul me away, it'll be a miracle," Jennifer said, double-bolting the door.

Gabby fell back against the wall, exhausted, coughing and spitting into a handkerchief. So much had happened that morning and her body could barely keep up. She studied the mix of anger and fear on Jennifer's face. Just when her granddaughter seemed to be turning some kind of corner. Gabby glanced away, her eyes falling on the photograph of Lili by the sea. Slowly Gabby began to nod as inspiration took root. Suddenly she knew exactly what to do.

"Thank you, Lili," she whispered, reaching for the phone.

19

Like two criminals on the lam, Gabby and Jennifer glanced around furtively before hopping in a cab and heading up Broadway. Frieda Steinberg was waiting outside her apartment building on 89th Street, her faded blue '87 Buick Skylark parked alongside. As Jennifer transferred the bags into the waiting vehicle, Frieda handed Gabby the key and hugged her tightly.

"This is so exciting. It's like *The Fugitive*," she whispered giddily, stealing a glance up and down the block. As Gabby slid into the driver's seat, Frieda raised her eyebrows. "You don't want you should have younger eyes behind the wheel?"

"The girl has been up all night," Gabby explained. "She could use a little sleep, Frieda. Thanks for this. You know I would normally never ask."

"What are you talking about, it sits in the garage like a widow. You know the feeling. Have a wonderful trip."

Gabby started the motor and the car

lurched forward. She slammed on the brakes and they screeched to a halt.

"You want to ease the brake on, Gabby," Frieda called through the window. "It's very sensitive. And don't have a heavy foot on the gas. There's a lot of life in her." Gabby nodded and pulled away. Before she knew it, she had gunned the car down the street, jolted it to a standstill, then bolted forward and around the corner.

"We're off," she told Jennifer, who nodded uncertainly.

Gabby pulled onto Riverside Drive and merged with the Henry Hudson Parkway. Jennifer glanced down at Gabby's feet. They barely reached the pedals. The lurching of the car was already making her sick. She had offered to drive, but Gabby maintained that Jennifer needed her sleep and the ride would go more smoothly when they got to the interstate. Jennifer observed her nana peering comically over the wheel, her face a study in concentration. But after the night she had had, she couldn't muster too strenuous a protest.

"Where are we going anyway?" Jennifer asked as she closed her eyes and snuggled into the cushiony flowered fabric of the passenger seat.

"Your mama and I, we loved doing this

when she was a young girl. While your papa Itzik was busy with the tailoring and the mending for his clients, we would play a little hooky from Lili's school and run away from the city. I thought maybe you and I could play a little hooky. Someplace no one can find us?"

Jennifer didn't really care where they were headed, just as long as she didn't have to go back to her father and the doctors in L.A.

"Well, the final destination is a secret," Gabby said with a mischievous grin. "But I can tell you that first we're heading north to the Berkshires. It's a little out of the way, but there's a town your mother and I loved to visit on our trips. We'd watch the leaves fall in October. We're a little late for that now. Oh, we'd sit outside the Red Lion Inn eating fresh pumpkin pie and talking about our dreams."

They were an hour or so outside Manhattan when Jennifer, who had been silent since conking out fifteen minutes into the trip, suddenly blurted out a remark that seemed to come from nowhere. "I don't have any dreams for myself. Not for a long time now," she said matter-of-factly, and went back to sleep.

Gabby pondered that remark during the rest of the drive into Massachusetts, wondering if the breakthrough she yearned to believe in for Jennifer was truly possible, wondering if her own failing physical condition would give her the time she needed to make one last journey, to lead her granddaughter back to health.

This was the dream that mattered now.

20

As twilight fell, they pulled into the quaint little town of Stockbridge, Massachusetts, checking into the Red Lion Inn, where Gabby had arranged for a room. The rambling white edifice, in continuous use since 1773, was exactly as Gabby had remembered it. The extensive history of the place gave it a sense of tradition she had long admired, the very life-affirming cornerstone the Nazis had tried to rip from her in the war. Those monsters had eliminated a people's connections to their families and their past, she insisted. And it was the importance of tradition that Gabby had pushed so hard on Lili, making her daughter's decision to relocate to the other side of the country particularly painful.

Gabby and Jennifer had dinner in the tavern at the back of the hotel, a charming setting marked by Staffordshire china, colonial pewter, and furniture reminiscent of the eighteenth century. Gabby's eyes lit up as she read to Jennifer the short history of the inn given on the back of the menu.

Gabby went on to read a list of the famous people who had stayed there over the years.

Jennifer listened politely, but even though she had slept nearly the whole trip between New York and Stockbridge, it had barely made a dent in her exhaustion. Further, the upsetting memory of the confrontation with her father earlier that day was still preoccupying her. She was also feeling betrayed. Why had Nana promised that she would return Jennifer to L.A. by Thanksgiving? It was a blow to the trust she'd begun to take for granted between them. Her thoughts turned to the previous night in the park. She had been so close to letting it all go. The truth of it was, nothing had really changed, had it? Not when the person closest to you was so willing to reject you. As Gabby chattered on, reading tidbits about the dining habits of Nathaniel Hawthorne, who had been a guest at the inn, Jennifer set about sampling every variety of Sam Adams the tavern had on tap.

After a scrumptious dinner of local favorites, including cider butternut squash bisque and grilled Yankee meat loaf, all of which Jennifer washed down with hearty pints of ale, Gabby took one look at her bleary-eyed granddaughter and knew it was time they retired for the night. Staggering up to their room on the second floor, Jennifer had trouble navigating the stairs. Gabby did her best to steady the girl but was forced to stand by helplessly as her granddaughter flopped down on the steps, bursting into howls of mindless laughter. With great difficulty, Gabby managed to half pull, half coax Jennifer back to her feet, up the stairs, and down the hall to their room. Opening the door, she couldn't keep herself from gently chastising Jennifer for trying to drown her emotions in alcohol.

"Emotions? What emotions?" Jennifer retorted with a giggle. But Gabby wasn't in the mood for laughing. It was time for a little straight talk.

"Listen to me, my granddaughter. You have that Prozac in you, on top of this you drink like a Russian captain. And when you do this, you no longer feel the world around you. You can't feel the one inside you either. You lose yourself, and when you do that, what have you got left?"

Jennifer shook her head with a silly grin as she opened the window wide, allowing cold air to come rushing in. "No, no, no, no, no, none of that psychological crap, Nana. The point is not to feel the world around me. Can you get that? Feeling too much is how I ended up in the park last night."

Gabby took off her wool sweater, closed the window, and turned to face her granddaughter, who had flopped down on the queen-size bed.

"Tomorrow's a new day, Jennifer. You can't be ready for it if you can't feel anything. Feelings are what is real. Some are bad, yes, but many are good. You have this place inside that tells you what is true and what is not. If you drown it with drink, it doesn't work."

Jennifer jumped to her feet and slammed the bathroom door. Gabby held her breath, unsure whether to check on her or leave her alone. She didn't have long to wait. Suddenly the door flew open with a force. Jennifer nearly banged her head on the low eaves of the ceiling as she reemerged, pointing a finger menacingly at her grandmother.

"Okay, let's be real. What does tomorrow have to offer someone like me? Tomorrow and the next day and the day after that? It's just a recycling of the same old shit right back through you, and you know what, it gets old."

"This is the beer talking," Gabby said, dismissing it with a wave of her hand as she went about unpacking her bag, pulling out a drawer of the antique oak dresser and filling it with her undergarments.

As Jennifer moved toward Gabby's side of the room she inadvertently knocked over a small table that held two crystal tumblers and a bottle of Perrier. The sound of glass shattering caused Gabby to jerk her head around in alarm, but Jennifer didn't miss a beat.

"See, that's where you get it all wrong. This is the real me. The one you want to send back at Thanksgiving, isn't that the arrangement? You and my father. 'Hey, Jennifer's too screwed up to run her own life. Let's make a deal!' Well, hey, Nana, the clock is ticking. Make your miracle."

"Jennifer, I promised you would go back to get your father to leave you alone. You know it's what we had agreed to back at the hospital or they might have locked you up right there. You saw what he was like, your father? I said what I had to say — so I could help you, sheyna."

"You want to help me? Then why the hell would you send me back? You're cutting me loose, Nana, aren't you? You're getting rid of me in twenty-four days. And if I refuse, it doesn't matter, does it? I heard what you told him: 'Do what you need to do.' "

"It was an expression," Gabby insisted as she nudged Jennifer aside in the close quarters at the end of the two beds. She got down on her hands and knees and carefully picked up shards of glass, placing them in a nearby wastebasket. "But, Jennifer," she continued, trying to suppress a stubborn cough, "you are not going to have to go back there to be in anyone's custody because you are going to be all right. You hear me? You will be in charge of your own life because you choose to be. You know how I know this?"

Gabby had cut her finger on a piece of crystal and now got to her feet, grabbing a wad of Kleenex to soak up the blood. She turned to face Jennifer and watched her as she pulled dried flowers from a dish of pot-pourri and tossed the buds one by one into the wastebasket. "I said, do you know how I know this, that you'll be all right, meydele?" Jennifer didn't reply, but her grandmother continued. "Because I know what you are made of. And in the shadow of death is no place for your precious spirit. You belong in the light."

Gabby stood there, breathing hard, her blood soaking through the tissue. Jennifer stared at her a moment, feeling a twinge of concern over her nana's cut that she quickly shook off. Instead, she flopped herself down on the dainty wooden rocker in the corner of the room. It looked frail enough to collapse.

"You know why I couldn't go through

with it in the park last night?" She rocked vigorously back and forth as if she might grind the chair into the smooth surface of the aged floorboards. Gabby looked at her. "Not because I couldn't feel my pain. No, that wasn't it. But because I let myself feel yours. Truth is, Nana, I don't live with your pain, all right? I live with mine. So I drink or whatever, so what? Give me a break."

There was a silence. Jennifer got up, threw herself on the bed, kicked off her shoes, reached for the remote, and clicked on the television. Gabby watched her lying there, drunk and ungrateful. She crossed to the television and switched it off.

"No," she announced quietly, "it's not all right."

Jennifer rolled her head, caught between the buzz from the alcohol and a conversation she didn't want to have.

"Look, Nana, you talk to me about your memories, about history, about who did what when as if any of this matters? Me, I prefer to self-medicate. Hey, I'm happy enough to go with you on this little trip of yours and I'm not going to hurt myself with you around, but don't ask me to reinvent the way I'm wired. This is who I am. Nobody ever wants to acknowledge who I am, least of all my family. Deal with it!"

Jennifer got up and, grabbing her back-pack, crossed to the seat on the windowsill. With her back to Gabby, she reached into the pack, finding the pills she'd stolen from Frieda Steinberg's medicine chest that day they'd gone for lunch. Her hand remained in the side compartment, fingering the bottle. She stared out at the trees. The wind blew hard, the sky gaping black.

"Would your mother have dealt with it?" Gabby demanded, refusing to surrender to the liquor talking. There was a pause and then Jennifer let go of the pills, turning from the window and kicking at the wall with a force that stunned Gabby. Her face contorted with the pain of the terrible accusation, she exploded.

"My mother left me to deal with all of this crap, don't you see that?"

Gabby stepped back as if she had been struck physically, barely able to contain her anger. "Shame on you! You blame your mother for her tragic death?"

"I blame everybody! They've all left me."

"Your mother loved you, Jennifer. She didn't choose to die like that."

"No? She was always letting her emotions get the best of her. I overheard the fight she had on the phone with my father that morning, screaming at him that he'd let me

153

down by not getting my car fixed on time. She was like a lion when she got angry. Always trying to protect me, and because of that, she never paid attention to what she was doing. Half the time she had her head in the clouds, dreaming how we could make things different. So emotional you could see her heart in her eyes. That's what emotions do for you, don't you see that? They steal your focus so that you can't see what's coming. Sixteen others saw that car and managed to get out of the way. She was either thinking about how mad she was at my dad or tearing up about my graduation. Either way it was her emotions that got her killed."

"How dare you say a thing like that," Gabby demanded. "You can't know what happened."

"What difference does it make? She's gone, gone, and I could never tell her what I needed to." Jennifer shook her head at the pain of it. "Never ask her the questions, never let her know how much it hurt to lose the one person who promised never to leave me. But she did. She did leave me. And you can't bring her back, so let's end this conversation, all right?"

Jennifer threw herself on her bed with a rage that no longer frightened Gabby but drew her forward to meet it.

"You have things to say to your mother, then say them. Don't keep them buried inside yourself."

"My mother's dead! Leave me alone."

"No, I won't leave you alone. When you love someone, you don't let them go on suffering on their own. Tell me what you've wanted to say to her. Let it go, Jennifer."

"You're not my mother, all right?"

"No, I'm not. But your mother is a part of who I am, just as she is a part of who you are."

"Stop it, Nana, don't do this," Jennifer shot back, burying her head under the pillow. Gabby wrenched it off her.

"I talk to your mother all the time because I can't bear her not being here with me. And I think it's good to talk to her. Because she's still alive inside me. And she's with us right now in this room. I know that."

"You're crazy, that's what you are!" Jennifer screamed back and moved away as far as she could get in the small confines of the room.

"Humor me. I won't be here that much longer and you'll do what you want. So tell me, what would you say to your mother if she was standing next to you, right here right now? What's to lose, Jennifer? Get it off of your chest. It's hurting you there."

"What do you know about what hurts me?"

"I don't know anything about what you've been through, Jennifer. That is true. Look at me. You think it's crazy that I speak to her? It's what we do when we lose those we love. It makes it bearable. At least for me." Gabby drew closer. "Go on, Jennifer, tell me what you would say to her if she was in this room. Because she is, meydele, she *is* here. Inside both of us. And I swear to God she's been waiting for you."

"This is too weird. What, we're going to speak to the dead now? I don't want to do this. Go away!" Jennifer said through gritted teeth. "Leave me alone!"

"I'm not leaving you, Jennifer, so talk to me!" Gabby pressed on, afraid of what she might be doing to her granddaughter but more afraid of losing her if she didn't push. "Talk to me. Tell me what's in your heart. Do it, Jennifer. Do it now."

"Stop it, Nana!" Jennifer screamed.

"*Now*, meydele, before you break into little pieces. Before you lose the part of your mother inside of you. Before you . . ."

"*Aahhh!*" Jennifer wailed, smashing her fist into the pillow and turning to look up at her nana, whose face shone bright with expectation.

"You've carried this pain too long now," Gabby pleaded with her. "Give it to me. Give me this pain inside your heart!"

And suddenly, clenching her fists, Jennifer exploded with a fury and a hurt that filled the room.

"Mom!" she cried, eyes closed with anguish. Gabby had no idea what to expect and held her breath. And then, like a dam bursting, Jennifer unleashed what was in her heart.

"You left me here alone. Why did you have to do that? Why didn't you look up, move faster, something!" she cried out.

Gabby stepped back, temporarily stunned by the force of Jennifer's plea. Then, hand to her heart, she opened her lips to respond, and it was as if Lili herself were standing there.

"It wasn't her fault. She never wanted to leave you, Jennifer, you know that."

Jennifer rose onto her knees, her face flushed with a mix of alcohol and rage.

"Why didn't she forget about my father? The way he hurt her, the women. Why didn't she care more about herself? She should have been more selfish, taken the car that day, let me walk, goddammit!" she spit out, eyes shut tight.

Gabby's face was also flushed. She shook

her head sadly. "She'd tell you you can't know what's going to happen in life, darling. She didn't mean to leave so suddenly. She'd tell you how sorry she was."

Jennifer leaped up, pacing the room in agitation. "Yeah, well, *sorry* doesn't cut it. We could have had more time together. I lost my father once and we both know he wasn't really very good at it. But it still hurt. And Mom was the only one I could count on, and then she left. If she hadn't stopped to buy that stupid book she would never have been in the wrong place at the wrong goddamn time. I needed her!"

Gabby stood her ground, quietly answering, "I know she'd say how sad it would make her to know she couldn't be there for you in the way that you wanted."

"What do you think it's like to put your mother in the ground one week before your senior prom?" Jennifer continued, lost in her pain. "To watch as they throw dirt on her coffin and your heart is ripped up because your world is broken forever and there's no fixing it?"

"It has to be terrible, Jennifer, this much I know."

"Not to even be able to show off for her in the dress that she helped me pick out . . . are you getting this?"

Gabby, trembling, nodded through her fear of what she had tapped into, her eyes trained on Jennifer, who continued prowling back and forth like an animal in a cage.

"And then the freakin' lunatics, these shrinks who got me hopped up on Xanax like it was God's gift and I didn't protest one little bit because, guess what, I *wanted* to go there."

"I understand, sweetheart."

"Do you really?" she shouted, turning now on Gabby as if she were indeed her dead mother, backing her up with every step forward.

"Do you know what it's like to finally trust again, to let a man into your most private places, and see him toss you out 'cause he can't get his shit together? You think you know what that's like, right? You do not!"

Jennifer was practically on top of Gabby, bearing down, possessed with an anguish that it hurt to part with, thrashing about as if she might harm her grandmother. Gabby withstood the onslaught, never once drawing back or averting her eyes.

"Say it, you haven't a clue, and Mom wouldn't either, 'cause she wasn't here and I could never tell her any of it. She couldn't even be here to hold me, just to hold me! Why? Why? Why live in a world where nothing's for certain, Nana? Where the men in your life leave 'cause they haven't grown up, where you can get nailed by a car crossing the street on account of some drunk driver's having a bad day. Why live in that kind of fucked-up world? Answer me! Can you do that? Answer me!"

At the height of Jennifer's rage Gabby opened her arms like wings of compassion. Slowly, tenderly, she wrapped them around her granddaughter, drawing her close, allowing her to pour her fury into her chest.

After several minutes, anger spent, Jennifer pulled back and stood in the middle of the room, arms lifeless at her side.

"You add it all up, you realize nothing matters, not anymore. Not me, not anything, and so you just, you know, let it all go. You just . . . let go." Her voice trailed off in resignation and acceptance. "I wanted so much, I wished to tell her . . . all of this. I tried. I didn't know how to." Her voice broke and her mouth formed a silent gaping wound, the loudest cry Gabby had ever heard.

For a long time Jennifer wept in her nana's arms, staring over her shoulder into the void.

Then, stroking her granddaughter's forehead gently, Gabby whispered into her ear.

"She's watched you, Jennifer, from where she is. She's held you when you were sleeping. You think she's left you, but she's still here. Not out in the world where you've been looking, but here, inside your heart. Your mom will never leave you, my sweet girl. If you look for her there, you will see she's never broken her promise."

Jennifer hugged her nana, her tears falling freely.

Gabby didn't know if in her mind Jennifer was hugging her mother or her grandmother just then. Maybe it didn't matter. Her precious granddaughter had, at least for now, come home.

Something from deep within Gabby now began to emerge. It was the story of her own pain. She knew she was the only one who could tell it. After she was gone, it would be lost forever unless she gave it now to Jennifer. She looked down at the trembling, vulnerable figure hugging her tightly. Gabby wondered if she dared place such a burden on a girl so frail. Like Lili, Jennifer had always objected to hearing about the Holocaust. But Gabby knew that this might be her only time to tell the tale. And this might be the only time Jennifer could truly hear it. Besides, it was all she had left to offer.

Gabby helped her granddaughter back

onto the bed, where Jennifer laid her head in her nana's lap. And there, over the sound of a brisk autumn wind rustling old New England shutters, Gabby set about relating the tale she knew Jennifer needed to hear, one that Gabby herself needed to tell.

21

"My little town of Zolynia in southeastern Poland was a lovely place to grow up. *Sheyn vi di zibn veltn,* beautiful as the seven worlds, my papa would say. We had nice schools, our friends were Jewish and gentile; Catholic, mostly. Papa was the local tailor. He could mend anything. Fania, your great-grandmother, was a musician and gave piano lessons to the local children whose families could pay for such things. In the summers we would play in the countryside with its big fields of hay and acres of wildflowers. And in the winter, when the town's little pond froze over, my sister, Anna, and I would take turns with the one pair of skates Papa could afford to get us. The two of us were on that ice until the sun went down."

Jennifer lifted her head, still weak from her emotional outburst and the large amount of beer she'd imbibed. "I forgot that you had a sister," she said.

"Anna." Gabby uttered the name with a sad twinkle of her eyes. "Oh, Anna could float on skates like she was born with them on her feet. She was a thing of beauty to watch." Gabby gazed mournfully into space. Jennifer looked up as silence filled the room, studying the pain lining her nana's face. "Go on, Nana," Jennifer whispered, her voice catching. "I want to hear it. I do."

Gabby gathered herself, nodding. "Yes, yes, I want to tell you . . ." and began again.

"It was on a cold September day when my whole world turned upside down. The leaves were already changing. The Nazis had been bombing Poland for two weeks. But we had word that the Polish army was fighting with great success. We didn't know the Russians had knifed us in the back, making a deal to split Poland with Hitler. When they swept into the country the Poles could not fight on both fronts. Zolynia ended up being on the side of the territory claimed by the Germans. We were afraid, but we had hopes the British or the French would come to our aid. We couldn't imagine that German soldiers would bother with our little town. That they would actually enter our homes was unthinkable.

"We were at the dinner table. Mama had made some sweets for my thirteenth birthday the next day, but Anna and I had begged so for a little taste that she gave in. She was serving a tiny chunk of babka with chocolate sprinkled on the top. It was my favorite. Suddenly there was a horrible noise and these men broke through our door. They were S.S., the most vicious of Hitler's army. They shouted at my father, pointing guns at all of us. Anna was screaming and Mama reached for her, but one of the men pushed her back against the piano. When she fell on it, there was this terrible sound, as if the piano itself were in pain.

"Papa yelled for my sister and me to run, to get away from this place, but the Germans were blocking the door. We didn't know where to go. They were turning chairs over, dishes were breaking, it was all happening so fast. Papa tried to pull my mother away from one of the men. She was beating his chest with her fists, screaming at him to leave her children alone and then . . . I don't know what happened. There were shots and Mama fell. Then I looked over and saw that Anna was covered in blood. She'd been hit in the shooting. I screamed as she collapsed next to my mother. They were both dead."

Gabby gripped her granddaughter's hand as she spoke of the horror. Burrowing deeper into her nana's lap, Jennifer squeezed back in response.

"In the next second, before they could turn their guns in our direction, I felt my father's strong hands grab hold of me. Then, out of nowhere, there was a pistol pointed at my father's head. Everything seemed to slow down for a moment, each split second a lifetime. I could see the gun. See my father's face. Feel the thunder of my own heart. And just as they were firing a bullet into Papa he was lifting me and with all his strength hurling me through the window behind him. All I could see was glass shattering all around me as I fell. And then time sped up. The next minute I was on the ground outside, bleeding, but alive. I ran from this place. I ran until the voices and the bullets had faded and I couldn't hear anything anymore." Gabby broke off.

"You must have been so afraid, Nana," Jennifer said softly. "Where could you go?"

Gabby nodded, shivering, pulling at a colorful patchwork quilt on the bed, tugging it over Jennifer and herself.

"I hid that night where a farmer had once kept his pigs and goats. Right there in the mud. You would have laughed at the sight of me if it weren't for the circumstances. I could see in the distance that many houses had been set on fire and I cried myself to sleep with thoughts of Papa, Mama, and dear Anna. The next day I ate the scraps the pigs were eating and at nightfall I escaped through the fields into the forest. I must have wandered for several days, drinking from puddles of rain and eating pinecones and wild mushrooms. I kept thinking that everyone I loved was gone."

Jennifer felt the tightening of her nana's grasp. She pressed Gabby's hand to her cheek protectively. The wind was howling outside, but Jennifer was lost in a world from the past, one that felt as if it were right there in the room with them.

"After many days, I had grown very weak; I had never known such cold. I couldn't see the point of going on any longer. I knew it was only a matter of time before they found me. I could hear shooting in the forest as Germans slaughtered Poles. I knew my fate was certain to be that of my family's. I decided then and there that I was going to die and there was no use hiding. With my parents gone, my sister, I was finished with this world, and I just wanted to get it over with. So I came out from behind the trees and bushes where I hid, walking in plain view where I'd be easily found, maybe shot right there like Papa and the others. It no longer mattered. I headed in the direction of the next village to turn myself over to the Nazis."

Jennifer sat up next to Gabby, her tears dried, her face sober, her eyes intent on her nana.

"I had been walking for several hours, and do you know what I thought of? Anna on those skates. I could think of nothing else right then except that I would never again see her on the ice, never hear her laughter, never feel her hand in mine as we hurried home for supper.

"I was lost, walking through the forest on my way to my death. And then I felt a tap on my shoulder. I turned to face a Polish woman, a gentile. What she was doing in the forest that day and at that moment I do not know. But this woman stopped me and suddenly she was shaking me, screaming into my face, 'Are you crazy? What are you doing here? Don't you know they will find you out here in the open?' I couldn't understand why she was so upset. What did it have to do with her? The next minute she was dragging me behind the trees so we wouldn't be seen. I told her everything that had happened to my family and to me. I thanked her for her concern but told her I no longer cared to live.

"This woman, she knew my father. She had seen me in his tailor shop. She insisted that I come home with her and said she would hide me. I thanked her and told her again that I didn't care to live. *Whack!*, she slapped me hard. I can feel it even now. She screamed at me, 'Foolish girl, don't you see it is not for you to throw away what your family was so desperate to have? You must choose life. You must live for those who had no choice.'

"And meydele, I don't know if it was the blow or the power of those words, but like that, I knew she was right. My father was a bear of a man, a heart the size of the forest. He would do anything to keep us alive. He had shielded me from the bullets, had literally thrown me from death's door. Yes, he would wish me to do anything to stay alive. So I followed this woman back to her home. There she hid me in her attic for nearly two and a half years."

"Two and a half! But Mom told me you escaped a death train. That partisans smuggled you out of the country?"

"That was later, after a suspicious neighbor, one sympathetic to the Nazis, nearly discovered my hiding place and I had to run into the countryside. No. For two and a half years this angel, Mrs. Pulaski, hid me, bringing me food in this little wooden bowl every morning and again at night. Bread and butter, a handful of oats in some cream when it was available, and for dinner — soup, a piece of potato or beets in it, a little meat if I was lucky.

"But, I did not do well in that attic. Mrs. Pulaski was a seamstress. People brought her clothing to mend. It's why she had come to see my father on a few occasions, to find stronger threads with which to do her work. Mrs. Pulaski said I could not make the slightest noise during the workday when persons would come and go. Many of her neighbors were willing collaborators and despised the country's Jews. If they discovered she was hiding me, Mrs. Pulaski would be shot and I would be sent to the camps.

"It was very cramped in that attic space. During the day I would cling to the slanted walls. This way my feet would not touch down on the floorboard. Hanging on, I would feel my knuckles turn white with pain. Many times they became so numb I could not feel them again for several hours. To occupy me, Mrs. Pulaski managed to get hold of scraps of old newspapers. These I nailed to the wall. I would read them while hanging there all day, sometimes twenty, thirty times, the same article again and again until I could repeat the words in my head. One day she managed to get hold of a book for me. It was a book on planting and farming I read so many times the pages fell out. In a short time I knew exactly how to rotate crops and what wheat grew best in cold weather, which of course was of absolutely no use whatsoever.

"I thought I would go crazy in that little attic. I often thought of escaping at night and taking my chances in the forest. I had heard from Mrs. Pulaski that many had been shot in this manner, but anything seemed better than the torture of silence, being forced to stay completely still for so many hours in this cage.

"It was after a particularly difficult day, what would have been my sister Anna's fifteenth birthday, that Mrs. Pulaski brought me my supper and found me shaking uncontrollably. I told her I couldn't stop thinking that my sister was dead and that it wasn't fair I should still be living. I said I couldn't bear to be in a prison any longer, each day darker than the one before. She held me and let me cry until there were no more tears. She wiped my eyes with her sleeve and held me close to her. 'There are times when it seems everything good in life has been taken from us,' she told me. 'Now is such a time. But I promise you, little one, if you open your eyes, your heart, you will find there are still gifts waiting for you each day. Sometimes it will not be an easy thing to see them,' she cautioned me. 'Sometimes you will have to work to find them.' "

Gabby brushed her hand softly on Jennifer's cheek, a faraway look in her eye. She smiled softly.

"What was she talking about, Nana? What kind of gifts could you find in that awful place?" Jennifer responded, shaking her head, confused.

"I hadn't the slightest idea what she meant either," Gabby gently replied. "Not at the time. But her words and her arms soothed me. That night I dreamed of Anna. Only, unlike many nights before, it wasn't a nightmare. In my dream we were both back on the ice on the pond in our village. Anna was flying by me, her head thrown back, laughing. When I woke up that next morning I remembered what Mrs. Pulaski had told me. That dream became my first gift."

"A dream?" Jennifer looked up at her grandmother.

"Yes." Gabby smiled, remembering. "Because that dream meant a piece of my sister from a happier time was still with me. That memory was better than a chicken dinner to someone starving like I was. The next day as I hung silently to the wall during the day-time hours, I noticed a pair of delicate wings opening and closing slowly just outside on the window ledge. I was amazed to see there a bright yellow butterfly, sunning itself. It stayed only a moment and then took off, soaring out of sight. That butterfly seemed like a treasure. It was so fragile and beautiful, and it reminded me that beauty still existed in the world, even with Nazis. After that, I made it my goal to find something like that to hold on to every day. Along with Mrs. Pulaski's kindness, it was how I survived all that time in the attic."

Gabby paused, rubbing her eyes with her hands, then gazed into the face of her granddaughter, whose expression was intense.

"What else did you find there, in your attic?" Jennifer asked quietly.

Gabby looked back at her wistfully. "Sometimes it was a glimpse of sunlight through the crack in the roof that made me feel better. A memory of my mother's cooking. The sound of rain tapping on the window or the sight of snow falling in the night. One winter's day I stared out at the icicles hanging by my window. I watched as they melted slowly in the sun.

"I don't know why, but I started to think of all the ways I looked at something as simple as water. It was in the tea my mother had waiting for my father every day after work. It was in the bath I used to soak in deliciously once a week, a pleasure forbidden to me in my hiding place. It was in the rain that gave us drinking water the year we had a drought, and it was in the form of the snowflakes I loved capturing on my tongue as a child. Water, I realized, could flow through my fingers, but it could come to me at another time transformed, allowing two sisters to soar along its frozen surface."

Jennifer shook her head, wiping away more tears, marveling. "You thought all of that about something like *water?*"

Gabby smiled. "When you have an endless amount of time on your hands, you'd be surprised at where your mind goes." Then she got a sad look on her face. "On the really hard days, I found the gift in realizing that someone like Mrs. Pulaski was still alive in the world.

"And ever since, even when I was forced to escape, when I was captured, when I jumped from a train and was smuggled to freedom, even then I continued to look for a gift, at least one each day. It helped to find the good in all that bad. Holding on to that good allowed the memory of my family to burn brighter than the fires of death that waited for me."

Gabby held Jennifer's tear-stained face in

her hands. "Your mother was that kind of good, that kind of light. And that same good and that same light is inside you, that much I know. You must only wish to find it there yourself." She kissed her upon the forehead. "There is a gift waiting for you each day, Jennifer. If you're willing to see it, hear it, even feel it, it's there."

Jennifer looked as if she would say something. Her eyes gazed deep into her nana's as if she were seeing her for the first time. And then Jennifer encircled Gabby with her arms and held on tighter than before.

Outside, the early November wind blew its promise of colder weather. The trees were in the process of losing their leaves. Through the front window Gabby could make out an old maple that, in the light spilling from the rambling porch, appeared on fire; she nodded at its offering, one last burst of autumn color.

22

The next morning Gabby watched in awe as Jennifer inhaled a hearty New England breakfast consisting of a short stack of blueberry pancakes, scrambled eggs, oodles of Vermont maple syrup, freshly made cranberry muffins, and several cups of Green Mountain coffee. She took this time to share with Jennifer their ultimate destination — Maine, a place she described as her favorite little corner of the world. Jennifer had never seen Maine, even though her mother had mentioned it over the years. The state seemed to hold a special place in her mother's heart and she had promised Jennifer they would visit there together one day, a promise she had not been able to keep.

After packing up the car, Gabby announced she had one stop she wanted to make before they set out on the road. A short time later, the two of them were standing in a room at the Norman Rockwell Museum. Gabby explained that this town had become the adopted home of the late

American illustrator, whose work was popular on magazine covers before, during, and after World War II. Rockwell had always depicted an idealized version of small-town America, a vision of what it hoped to be and sometimes was: a place where the simple joys in life were celebrated, like discovering first love, slurping malts at the local pharmacy, or playing baseball.

Gabby steered Jennifer toward the center room of the museum. In front of them were the four paintings she wanted Jennifer to see. They were representative of the ideals Gabby had sought out after the war. These paintings were based on a speech given by President Franklin Roosevelt outlining the Four Freedoms to which every human being was entitled: freedom from want, freedom of worship, freedom of speech and expression, and finally, freedom from fear.

The fourth painting seemed to make the greatest impression on Jennifer, with its depiction of a mother and father tucking their daughter safely into bed, sheltering her from the worrisome headlines of war found in the newspaper in the father's hand. She lifted her camcorder and recorded a few seconds of the touching scene before a guard reminded her that no filming was allowed.

Later, traversing the Massachusetts Turnpike en route to Boston, Jennifer thought of the monsters who had murdered members of her family in Poland. In that one horrible act they had stripped her nana of her parents, her sister, and her freedom from fear. They had stolen Gabby's sense of place and destroyed her innocence, leaving her with two choices: to give up and accept death or to fight for her life. Jennifer looked over at her nana asleep in the passenger seat. Her grandmother had been coughing a lot during the night. Jennifer was suddenly and keenly aware that in taking this trip, even in her poor health, Gabby was once again choosing life. Furthermore, she was choosing to affirm Jennifer's life.

The immensity of that gift shook Jennifer to her roots. Reaching over with one hand, she pulled the blanket of an overcoat up over her nana's chest.

Jennifer had a sudden wave of longing to speak with her mother, to tell her about this trip and Nana's story about the gifts, and to ask why her mother had never shared it. She thought she probably knew what her mother would answer to that question; after all, it was her nana's story to tell. She wanted to ask her mother what she ought to be doing for Gabby, how she might ease her suffering. And then, as she recalled the memory of her attempted suicide on a California beach, she had an irresistible urge to feel her mom once more tucking her into bed the way she had every night throughout Jennifer's childhood.

Remembering her mother's tragic death filled her with sadness. Her mom had deserved more from life. Yet Jennifer suddenly became aware of another feeling surging within her, one she hadn't felt for a very long time — gratitude. She was filled with a profound appreciation for all her mother had given her, for the way she had lived and struggled and persevered. She had been unselfish, planning and working for Jennifer's future, a future she couldn't know she would never be a part of. Except her mother *was* a part of it. As her nana had said, and as Jennifer could now feel acutely, her mother was right there inside her.

And with a heart full of memory and a soul suddenly filled with thanksgiving, Jennifer spoke in a voice she immediately recognized from another time in her life, a period when she had known she was safe and nourished and loved. "Thank you, Mom," she whispered as Nana stirred a little nearby. "For everything."

23

It was a few hours before Gabby awoke, sleepily squinting at the sunlight pouring through the window. To her surprise she found they had left Massachusetts and were nearly through the brief snippet of coastal New Hampshire ending at Portsmouth.

"How you doing, sleepyhead?" Jennifer teased.

"That was some *shlof*," Gabby said, wiping the sleep from her face.

"You had a good rest. You needed that," Jennifer said, an odd smile on her face that did not escape Gabby's attention.

"You seem in a strange mood, meydele," Gabby said, sitting up. "Happy, I think they call it. Did I miss something?"

"Not much," Jennifer tossed back playfully. "Just forest after forest of burnt orange and golden leaves saying good-bye for the season, a huge flock of Canada geese heading south for the winter. I just had to pull over and film them. You, of course, never woke up. Oh, yeah, and a flasher on the side of the road just outside of Boston, but in his case you really didn't miss much."

Gabby nodded appreciatively, grinning. "She has a sense of humor, this one. Who knew?"

A sign up ahead heralded their entrance into Maine. Gabby cheered, lifting her arms in triumph. Soon Jennifer had followed suit, lifting one hand in the air, the two hooting it up like a couple of beer-toting football fans until the car threatened to detour down an embankment and Jennifer was forced to return both hands to the wheel.

"I used to come here as often as we could when your papa Itzik was still living," Gabby said. "He loved it as much as I did. When your mama turned ten we started making our own little trip, just the two of us, once a year."

"When I was a kid I remember her saying that she loved California but that nothing was as pretty as the coast of Maine. It didn't really mean anything to me."

"Because you never experienced it for yourself, young lady. Trust me, we get to Bar Harbor, you are going to fall in love."

"I never really knew Papa Itzik. He died when I was so little."

"Yes, Jennifer, but he knew *you*. It meant so much to him, knowing you were here in this world; knowing that a piece of his family, a piece of him would remain and continue when he was gone. He went too soon, my Itzik. Sixty-two, meydele. That's too young. He deserved more years."

Gabby observed the sadness that had come over Jennifer at this last remark. Then it struck her. "I didn't mean . . ."

"It's all right, Nana."

"Of course your mama of all people should have been blessed with more years. I would gladly have traded —"

"It's all right, Nana, really," Jennifer insisted again, attempting to smile. She remembered her mother at forty-four, her beautiful auburn tresses, the glow in her eyes when she became excited. Jennifer chose to concentrate on that as she drove across the state line into Maine.

They pulled into a roadside restaurant that featured home cooking. Over fresh cod and chips and blueberry cobbler, Gabby told Jennifer anecdotes about her grandfather. How he would bounce her on both of his knees, turning his glasses sideways to coax her laughter. The way he loved playing peekaboo with her when he and Gabby last visited California just before he took ill. Gabby recalled how Lili had brought Jennifer east to visit him in the hospital;

even Barry had cut short a business trip to join them a day later.

"What did you think of my father back then?" Jennifer asked.

"Listen, I didn't like the way he would rush here and there to make his Hollywood deals, leaving you and your mother on your own. But your papa Itzik, he thought your father was a good provider and that the bills would get paid and you would all have enough to live on. That was the important thing."

Jennifer was quiet for a moment, digging into her cobbler. She looked wistfully at her nana. "You miss him a lot, don't you?"

"Your papa?" She smiled longingly, as if she could see him right there next to her. "Every day," Gabby said, taking a long sip of her hot tea that she cradled in her hands to warm them.

"How *did* you meet?" she asked, truly wanting to know everything.

Gabby looked up, grinning with remembrance. "On a train," she said, her face growing solemn recalling the moment.

Jennifer was thunderstruck as it dawned on her: "You mean *that* train?"

"Yes, meydele." Gabby nodded, touched by Jennifer's keen interest. "A nosy neighbor kept coming by, snooping around

Mrs. Pulaski's house while I was up in that attic. I was sure I would soon be discovered. I couldn't risk them finding me there, jeopardizing the life of the angel who had hid me. So I fled. Later, with a handful of others, I was captured in the forest searching for the partisans, the freedom fighters. We were placed on a train I later found out was bound for a death camp named Belzec.

"You hear that people in these cars were stuffed in like cattle, but it was worse. We could barely breathe in there from people having to relieve themselves on top of one another. Some were dying or were already dead, we couldn't know from what was happening. It was dark, inhuman. For some reason, the train would slow down every so often, we didn't know why. A day after we had boarded, some men around me managed to break open the large wooden door. It was late afternoon, the sun close to setting; and at that moment, the train began slowly rolling once again. Some of us slid the door open a crack for a little air. Suddenly I felt this hand on my back, shoving me forward. Before I could turn around to see who was doing this I was pushed from the moving train. Then I heard gunshots going off and I was certain others were jumping from this train and God knows how many the Nazis were stopping, but I didn't look back, I just kept tumbling down the hill, cutting myself everywhere. And then I came to a stop. I could feel my heart going through the roof of my mouth, but I didn't see any soldiers. Like a miracle, I was alive. It was the second time I had been thrown free of death.

"In the next few seconds this wild-looking man came crashing down the hill right behind me. He had been the one pushing me from the train. We looked at each other, then back up the hill. There was silence. The train was already gone. There were no others. Any who might have attempted to leap to freedom were either dead or driven back into the hellhole from which we had just come. We alone had escaped.

"When we got back our breath we ran into a field, hiding beneath fresh-cut bales of hay. We smiled the smile of the living, silently searching each other's face. He had the most beautiful brown eyes and I could now see, even with his face smudged with dirt and his hair matted, he was a nice-looking young man. We ran all night to find the resistance fighters. I was so weak he had to carry me half the time, and he did so without complaint. We spent several days searching. I felt close to giving up, but this young man told me we were going to be rescued. Of this he was certain. We fell in love almost instantly. After five days we found a group of partisans and were smuggled first to Sweden, then to Scotland, where we lived for the remainder of the war. That young man who threw me from the train and carried me through the forest was your papa. We were married in Edinburgh in 1945 and came to America soon after. I was eighteen."

Jennifer drank in every word of her nana's astonishing story. "I cannot believe I never heard any of these tales."

"Your mother felt these stories would disturb you. She told me once she had meant to tell you these things, but with the divorce and the changes in your family life, she thought such information would do nothing but add to your nightmares. After all, these horrible things from the war did not make for pleasant conversation. Also, I think Lili had her own problems being the daughter of survivors. This I may have contributed to. I always believed in telling the truth about what had happened, all of it, even when she was very little. Others would hide it from their children, but for some reason — maybe it was selfish — I shared too much with your mother when she was too young to hear it. I believe this she held against me. Maybe I gave her too much worry."

Gabby turned away, shaking her head at the memory of it. Jennifer could see the guilt her nana was carrying and reached out a hand to comfort her.

"I'm glad I've heard it from you, Nana. It's like a piece of a puzzle you never knew was missing, but when you find it, you know just where it belongs. Does that make sense?"

Gabby nodded and started to cough. Her coughing grew so loud and persistent that the waitress came over and asked if there was anything she could do. Gabby stubbornly waved her off, drinking some water while holding up a palm to a deeply concerned granddaughter, which, translated, meant she shouldn't go anywhere or call anyone.

"I've been hearing this cough get worse and worse, Nana. Why won't you let someone help you?"

"I am," she said, catching her breath. "I wanted to go to Maine with my granddaughter and you've brought me here. That's the help I need right now. Now tell the truth — that was some cobbler!"

Her eyes somehow managed to twinkle, even through the pain. Jennifer now saw who her mother had inherited her brave face from, her ability to sparkle during tough times.

That night, as they lay awake in their beds in a rustic motel outside of Freeport, Gabby asked Jennifer the question she always put to herself before she went to sleep: *What was the gift today?*

Jennifer responded with a list: the last vestiges of autumn colors she'd witnessed on the drive through New England, the magnificent formation of geese winging their way to safety, Rockwell's illustrations of the Four Freedoms.

"But if I had to pick one, Nana, it would be your giving me a past, one with a love affair between two people that lasted a lifetime."

"Thank you for that," Gabby said softly, and Jennifer thought she could hear tears in her voice.

"And yours, Nana?" Jennifer wanted to know as the moon shone through the window, bathing the two of them in celestial illumination.

"My gift from this day?" Gabby paused, taking in a deep breath that she seemed to savor.

"This moment, sheyna," she said happily. "This moment will do just fine."

24

For the next three days the two women toured the picturesque seaports of Boothbay Harbor, Rockland, and Camden. They sampled food as if eating had just been invented — strolling along the ocean nibbling on fresh-baked pretzels, settling into the cozy corner of a diner to devour the fresh catch of a local fisherman, tasting heavenly homemade desserts by a roaring fire. Throughout their culinary and sightseeing tour, Gabby regaled Jennifer with details of her past: visits she had made to Maine, both alone with Itzik and then, when Lili came along, those the three of them enjoyed together. She tickled Jennifer with memories of her mom as a rowdy teenager, and with tales of the fun and predicaments they encountered on their annual mother-daughter getaway, a just-us-girls caper by the sea.

Recalling one such trip, Gabby suggested they relive one of Lili's favorite activities — an afternoon excursion aboard the hundred-and-thirty-year-old Belfast-

Moosehead Railroad. The historic train wound through lovely countryside, past the last of the crisp colored autumn leaves slipping off the graceful branches of their moorings. They chugged along inlet streams and crystal blue lakes, Jennifer training her camcorder on the glorious scenery. En route, they savored hot apple cider stirred by cinnamon sticks while a trio of musicians entertained them with Celtic and American folk songs. Gabby, inspired by the raucous atmosphere and the heartening changes she saw in her granddaughter, piped in with a verse of "O Danny Boy" that had Jennifer and fellow tourists rolling on the floor. Gabby's interpretation of the well-known Gaelic anthem had a distinctive *Fiddler on the Roof* tone.

They had been on the road a week, and at the end of each new day they continued the ritual Gabby had introduced, sharing with each other the gifts the past twenty-four hours had offered. There was the single perfectly burnished maple leaf that had floated onto Gabby's lap as she sat on a bench overlooking the harbor. In Owl's Head one evening the golden orb of a full moon became the gift at the top of that day's list. A stroll by the sea one day had evoked a memory of Lili singing Jennifer a lullaby by the ocean on the other coast. On still another day, Gabby witnessed an old man kissing each finger on the hand of his little grandchild. The two of them would often press their heads close together on the edge of the bed at night, delighting in the playback of sights and moments Jennifer had captured that day on her camcorder.

At the end of the week Gabby and Jennifer decided to rest up for their final destination, Bar Harbor. They lounged in their comfortably rustic room, doing little but napping, reading, and eating. At the end of the day, as the nightly ritual began, the two of them lay silent in the darkness of the room. Jennifer thought and thought but hadn't a clue of where to begin.

"Absolutely nothing happened today, when you think about it," she remarked, laughing at how lazy they'd both been. "We didn't go anywhere, didn't do anything. Hmm. You know, maybe some days you just don't find the gift. That's not so terrible, is it, Nana?"

Gabby was getting drowsy but didn't miss a beat. "Start at the top of the day, Jennifer, we'll find it."

Jennifer exhaled sharply. "All right, suit yourself. Let's see, we got up . . ."

"Stop right there," Gabby said, yawning.

"What?" Jennifer said, confused.

"You said we got up, right?" Gabby stretched, fixing her covers, fluffing her pillow.

"Yeah, we got up," Jennifer repeated. She was confused. "So?"

Gabby grinned as she turned onto her side. "Sometimes, meydele," she whispered softly, "that's gift enough."

Jennifer lay in her bed considering her nana's words. She thought back to something her mom had told her a short time after the divorce, when Jennifer found her crying in her bedroom. Her tears had shaken Jennifer and she fearfully asked if the divorce had made her mom feel like giving up on living. The question shocked Lili and she had quickly dried her eyes, pulling Jennifer tightly to her. "Listen to me, Jennifer, and remember this always. Each day is a gift. And Jen, even with the pain, I'm thankful for each and every one." Her mother had tried to get her to see that truth. And what had she done?

Years later, on a beach one night at sunset, she had ended up turning her back on this truth. Her nana had been trying to deliver the same message. It was only now, having faced the worst of her pain, that Jennifer was finally able to hear a voice that had been inside her all along. Only at this moment did she truly comprehend the meaning of her mother's words.

She thought about the pills she had swiped from Frieda. They were still in her backpack, an exit plan if she needed one. They now seemed a vivid reminder of what it was like to live a life without realizing its gifts. You had to be asleep to miss it all.

Jennifer's thoughts were interrupted by her nana's sudden coughs. The coughing became so violent that Gabby withdrew to the bathroom. Jennifer listened to the noise from the other side of the door. *Why did the women in her life have to suffer so?* she thought sadly.

In the darkness, with the sound of her nana's heartrending struggle in her ears, Jennifer found herself offering up a prayer. And for the first time in a long time, it was not an anguished appeal to end a life but a heartfelt plea to sustain one.

25

Driving into Bar Harbor along a road lined with stone walls and trees that led into the village, Jennifer could instantly see what had drawn her grandparents there over the years. Extending into the Atlantic from its rocky coast and dotted by historic Victorian homes, Bar Harbor was laced with the old world, the refined, and the utterly charming.

A hundred years earlier, its soaring granite cliffs had been the playground of America's business tycoons. Vestiges of their largesse could still be found sprinkled throughout the locale. One readily glimpsed the gilded hand in the impressive architecture of several of the town's more imposing residences. And in neighboring Acadia National Park, carriage paths, designed by John D. Rockefeller, Jr., for the rich and famous, were still in use, adapted for the modern era so that bicyclists and hikers of all ages and from all parts of society might enjoy them. All in all, Bar Harbor was a lovely, tasteful village, full of a rugged New

England beauty in its location on Maine's coast.

Gabby seemed in particularly good spirits after a difficult night spent as much in the bathroom as in her bed. She was brimful of anecdotes, familiar sights touching off memories within her like mental fireflies. Over there at the park's swings a then-six-year-old Lili's ice-cream cone had melted all over her new dress. She had been inconsolable until a new treat had rescued the day. On that corner by the Starbucks, which used to be a dress shop, Jennifer's papa had surprised Gabby by having a driver pick them up in a horse and carriage. To her utter delight, they were then taken on a sunset ride along the bay. It had been their tenth anniversary, they most certainly couldn't afford it, but Itzik had insisted that "for just one night, let's see what it feels like to be Rockefellers."

They spent the morning exploring the quaint, delightful boutiques dotting the promenade at the water's edge, later enjoying a lunch of lobster bisque and hand-carved turkey sandwiches with fresh cranberry relish that was as delicious as Gabby had remembered. In the afternoon they drove to the summit of Cadillac Mountain, where together they admired the vista of evergreen tree-covered hills spilling into the ocean on which sailing ships and yachts bobbed. Jennifer marveled at her nana's energy. She was still game for drinking it all in, even after her difficult bout with coughing the night before. To realize that she came from such remarkable stock struck Jennifer as one of the greatest of gifts, one that her mother, she realized, had replicated in attitude and passion if not in length of years.

Later, over tea and popovers at Jordan Pond House, a local tradition Gabby explained, the ebullient elderly woman reached into her bag and pulled out a little box.

"When did you have time to find this?" Jennifer grinned with surprise as she carefully unfolded the yellow tissue in the box.

"This morning. The saleslady in the local handicrafts shop was talking your ear off about puffin- and whale-watching. I saw it sitting on a mantel over the fireplace. As I got closer I heard it whispering: 'All right, lady, I'll make you a deal. You take me off this shelf, I'll make your granddaughter a first-rate present.' "

Jennifer pushed the tissue aside and turned the gift over. It was a small leather-bound book, its edges trimmed in gold leaf, a length of blue ribbon emerging as a place-finder from between its pages. Inlaid in the handcrafted cover was a richly textured needlepoint. But it wasn't just the fine artistry of the stitches that struck her. It was the subject matter. For the threads on the canvas in the center of the book depicted the flight of a delicate yellow-bodied butterfly, its multicolored wings spread gloriously wide, as if offering an embrace. Jennifer remembered Gabby's story of the delicate butterfly that had come to rest outside the window of Mrs. Pulaski's attic. How it had given her nana hope and beauty at a time when she had little. She sat back now, moved at the sight of it.

"It's a journal, Jennifer," Gabby said excitedly. "The pages are empty. They wait for you to fill them, to tell about the gifts you will find each day, in the future that also waits for you." Gabby leaned closer. "Maybe, when you are going through a difficult time — and such days are part of the challenge we get to face in living — you will take out this book and read what you have already written. It will remind you that while there is darkness, you also have good, beauty, light, and rich memories to cling to." She looked at Jennifer now with a glowing smile. "The pages are blank, yes, because they are like you, sheyna meydele . . . filled with possibilities."

Jennifer cradled the journal in her hands, a single tear trailing down her cheek. "I don't know what to say, Nana. It's the most beautiful thing imaginable."

"Now there I must disagree," Gabby replied, brushing her fingers against her granddaughter's hand. "*You* are the most beautiful thing imaginable. Believe that always; keep it in your heart. And know that wherever you are, when you feel that beauty spreading its wings within you, somewhere there will be an old woman clapping her hands and laughing."

Jennifer wiped away her tear, nodding. Gabby drew back, her smile slowly fading away, replaced with an odd sort of solemnity.

"Now, there is something you must help me do before we return to New York," Gabby said, bringing Jennifer up short.

"Return to New York?"

Jennifer had completely lost track of time. It hit her suddenly that she would be forced to leave her nana in two brief weeks. Suddenly the reality of all that awaited her back in L.A. came crashing down on her. She could feel the weight of facing her father, the unsettling necessity of having to make choices for the life for which she had not planned to make plans.

Jennifer might have remained preoccupied with these depressing thoughts had it not been for her nana's hacking cough, which reclaimed her attention. The cough seemed even more labored than on previous occasions. But before she could speak, Gabby was already in action.

"We must go now, meydele, come," Gabby said, her voice filled with urgency as she struggled to get to her feet. "You must take me there now, please."

Jennifer rose immediately, startled at this sudden reversal of direction. What could her nana possibly have to do here in such a hurry? Bewildered, she nevertheless assumed Gabby had her reasons, helping her out to the car and into the front seat.

Jennifer had no idea what she was about to encounter, nor that her nana's unusual behavior had little to do with her and everything with events that had occurred decades earlier and half a world away.

26

Driving to the footpath overlooking the ocean took no time at all. Gabby tossed out directions in between spasms. Parking the car on the gravel-filled shoulder, Jennifer helped her nana up to a dramatic promontory some fifty yards ahead. Deeply concerned about Gabby pushing herself beyond her limit, Jennifer nevertheless wished to honor her nana's desire to reach a destination that appeared to be of great importance to her. With great care, Jennifer doggedly led Gabby along the footpath up the hill. After some climbing, the two arrived at a massive rock formation jutting out into the sea. They followed the path across to it as Jennifer nervously eyed her nana to see how she was holding up.

The wind had died down over the last few hours, but it was still brisk and Jennifer was grateful Gabby had insisted that they both wear gloves and hats. She looked out at the Atlantic and a blanket of clouds forming overhead that might prove threatening given time. Still, it was a magnificent view. This was clearly a place of great sentimental value to her nana, and Jennifer had to admit she was pleased Gabby wanted so badly to share it with her. Jennifer turned to her nana to tell her so but stopped short. Gabby stood tall, her eyes shut, and in her hand she clutched something tightly to her chest.

"What is it, Nana?"

Without opening her eyes, Gabby smiled weakly and answered, "Where we are has always been special to me, Jennifer. Your papa and I married just before the boat sailed for America. After a year of working, your papa read about this lovely little town by the sea. He announces to me that we have never had a proper honeymoon. The next thing I know we're on our way to Maine. I had never even heard of the place." Gabby began coughing, opening her eyes now, fighting the pain in her lungs.

"Nana, let's go back. You shouldn't be out here," Jennifer insisted. But Gabby held out her hand so that Jennifer might help her sit. Jennifer took off her own scarf, wrapping it around her nana's neck, and bundled her grandmother's coat around her as best she could.

"It was a Saturday evening. We had taken a train and two buses to get here. When we arrived, Itzik insisted on seeing everything.

We walked along this very same path and somehow found ourselves out here on this rock, looking across the ocean, back toward Europe, toward all the sadness we had left behind. He promised me that the rest of our lives we would never have to know such heartbreak. Then he got down on one knee and told me he loved me and that he would guard me like this rock that stood guard over the ocean."

Jennifer turned to her, visibly moved. "Nana, that is so romantic. You are so lucky to have had a man who cared for you that much."

"Yes, yes, I was. And he was true to his word, my Itzik. Soon he'd left the bakery job he had on Orchard Street and went to work in the shmatte business, ladies' clothes, moving them from one store to another. There he met a nice man who cut the cloth, and this man taught him a few things, and then you know what?"

"Yes, he became a tailor."

"Like my father. So life is interesting."

Gabby still held what was in her hand closely to her chest. Jennifer wanted to ask her about it, but the sadness in her nana's eyes led her not to.

"You say how lucky I was to have such a man. And it's true. But luck, darling, can also be a burden." Jennifer watched as Gabby got a faraway, anguished look in her eye. "Itzik would tell me I must stop blaming myself for having been lucky enough to have survived the murders in my house, but I could never help it."

"But why? It wasn't your fault, Nana." Jennifer was taken aback. She had never had the slightest indication that her nana was carrying such guilt for being alive.

"It was never about fault, Jennifer. We feel guilty when we don't think we are deserving of a reward or when we have caused harm to others. Yes, I had learned about the true gifts life gives us each day. Gifts of love I learned also from my Itzik. But never did I stop believing that it should be Anna enjoying all these treasures. What would her daughter or son have looked like? I asked myself. Where would she have built a home? Would she have continued skating?" She paused, stifling a cry in her throat, coughing instead as she peered out over the ocean. "I think so, yes. She would be skating in Central Park today had she lived instead of me."

"But, Nana," Jennifer pleaded with her, "why couldn't it have been *both* of you who lived? Why must you feel guilty that it was only you?"

"Because it was one or the other," Gabby

insisted, her eyes brimming with the hurt of this terrible memory. "If she had been closer to Papa when the Nazis arrived at our dinner table, it would have been Anna who escaped through the window, not me!"

Jennifer could find no words of comfort. Her heart beat in tune with her nana's suffering.

"It is like a knife cutting away pieces of me from the inside, my dear granddaughter. It will not make sense to you. It never did to Itzik or to Lili, this I know. I think your mother moved so far away because she couldn't bear to see it. But my beautiful sweet sister died and I alone lived. And this guilt has burned in me until this day."

Jennifer pulled some tissues from her pocket, helping to wipe the tears from her nana's eyes.

"Itzik tried hard to remove these thoughts from my mind, but at this and this alone, he failed. When he died, I came back to this place and it became my rock of sadness, on which I grieved. He promised me no more tragedies, no more heartache. But he was a better tailor than a prophet, I'm afraid." She smiled sadly, holding the object in her hand tighter still.

"When your parents divorced, I came here to cry for my sweet Lili and for you,

Jennifer. When my sweet daughter, your mother, was killed by that drunk driver I came back here to grieve. I remember calling out from here to my sister, letting her know that maybe she was lucky in some way, too, never having had to bury a daughter."

Jennifer reached for her nana's hand and held fast. Gabby looked into her eyes, a sad smile on her lips. The wind whipped up, bringing the taste of salt water to their lips.

"I tried desperately to reach you, to spend time, but you were always so busy. I thought to myself, *It's good. She has a life, Gabby. Leave her alone.*"

"Nana, I'm sorry, I didn't realize —"

"No, no, no, it's all right. We must all grieve in our own way. But then, when the call came from your father a few weeks ago, saying they had found you on this beach and you were . . ." She emitted a muffled cry and covered her mouth with the back of her trembling hand. "I thought my God, it will be too much for me to bear." She wept, again closing her eyes as if to gather her strength.

Jennifer cried quietly beside her, the sound of the water smashing against the rocks below growing louder and more vigorous. The sun was dipping in and out of the clouds and Gabby's tears glistened gold as they caught the light. After a few moments, Gabby let out a long sigh, nodding with acceptance as she composed herself and looked into her granddaughter's eyes.

"Listen to me, meydele. What I found in these short weeks of time we have been together is that the tragedy of losing you has changed into an opportunity to grow closer to you, to find out who you really are. You were the light in the darkness to me. I needed to come here now, to be here with you, Jennifer, so that this rock would not forever be linked to tears, but so that it could once again be a place of forgiveness and of hope."

The wind tugged on her now, but Gabby braced herself. Slowly she opened her hand. Jennifer could see two small plastic containers lying side by side, one clear, the other tan. She observed that the clear vial seemed to contain what looked to be earth. Turning her attention to the tan bottle, Jennifer froze. The cold brisk wind seemed to move up her backbone, chilling it from the inside out. She immediately recognized one of the vials of Valium she'd stolen from Frieda Steinberg's medicine cabinet.

"I realize now that to go on, to live life with all you deserve, you must forgive yourself for having chosen death over life. But I also realize that if I am asking you to do this, I must be willing to forgive myself for doing the reverse."

Jennifer watched, confused, thrown off balance by the sight of these pills she thought her nana had not known about. Trembling, she was ashamed at the sight of them now. Gabby opened the two bottles and then reached out as Jennifer helped her to her feet.

"I am not so religious as we once were in Poland, but we had a ceremony, a ritual tied to the New Year holiday of Rosh Hashanah. We would go down to the river to throw away our sins. *Tashlich,* they called it."

"Yes." Jennifer nodded, remembering. "Mom and I did that a few times with friends when I was young. I remember throwing bread crumbs from Venice Beach."

The two exchanged a look of recognition at the mention of that location. Gabby nodded sadly. Jennifer bit her lip at the memory of the last time she had been on that beach.

"So, meydele," Gabby said gently. "What do you say we make our tashlich together? You with your pills, which somehow managed to find their way onto this trip." She smiled sadly, searching Jennifer's troubled eyes. "Me with this little bit of dirt I took from Poland many years ago. Somehow I thought it would keep Anna closer to me. But it's done nothing but serve as a guilty reminder that I walked away from death when she could not."

Facing the water, Jennifer took in the sight of her nana, her head bent as she whispered something over the bottle she held. Jennifer shook at the deep emotion filling her nana's face. She held her breath as Gabby pulled her arm back and with all of her strength cast the contents of her bottle out over the water. Gabby held her hands aloft a moment in a gesture of farewell, and Jennifer marveled at the conviction she saw in her grandmother's face and the air of liberation that seemed to surround her.

Gabby turned to Jennifer, her face reddened from the cold. She had no idea what her granddaughter would do now. This was her decision. Jennifer felt the weight of the moment and her nana's eyes. She knew in her heart that she had turned her back on the gifts her mother had given her, those of her nana, maybe even something from her father. Suddenly she remembered the dream she'd had when she was in the hospital. Her mother had been standing on a rock throwing something into a body of water. Jennifer looked up at her surroundings. Yes, she told herself with amazed recognition, *this* was the place she'd seen.

Jennifer stared down at the pills, then squeezed the vial in her hand and turned to face the water.

Gabby watched silently as Jennifer rocked back and forth on her heels, lost in her thoughts. Jennifer's face filled with concentration and Gabby could swear she was now speaking to someone else who wasn't there. *But yes,* Gabby thought as the wind whipped in her ears, *I do indeed sense Lili's spirit.* And then Gabby felt her breath catch in her throat as, with a cry of release, her face ablaze with certainty and strength, Jennifer hurled the pills out into the ocean.

The two stood quietly side by side for a few minutes, neither one wanting to break the spell of this sacred moment.

"Look beneath your feet, meydele," Gabby whispered finally.

Jennifer looked down, noticing for the first time the deep network of fissures crisscrossing the rock on which they were standing.

"This rock has seen many storms. Here it stands exposed to the elements, covered with the scars of its past. But one thing that always gave me comfort in coming here — it has not crumbled. It is still standing at the water's edge, facing the wind and the sea and whatever the future will bring."

Gabby put her arm around Jennifer's waist, smiling up at her. "Our hearts are like this rock. They will not crumble as long as we live and as long as we love."

Gabby then reached up and placed her hands on Jennifer's head in an act of silent blessing. And then, as if it were the most natural thing in the world, Jennifer did the same, her palms gently touching down upon the head of her nana.

The two stood, sanctifying each other amid the wind and sea, amid hope and forgiveness, and it felt to Jennifer as if time itself were suspended. That she could feel not only her nana's touch at this moment, but her mother's as well.

And then it happened. It was so swift, the previous moments so full of power and emotion, that Jennifer was caught unawares. Like an unexpected flash of lightning in a sea of gathering clouds, Gabby suddenly collapsed.

Jennifer cried out in horror. Immediately she sprang into action, catching her nana's frail body. Jennifer felt Gabby's weight sink into her arms and nearly cried at the sight of her nana's head rolling weakly against her own chest. Jennifer knew she had to get her off this rock and to a hospital as quickly as possible.

Lifting her nana into her arms, Jennifer made her way down the footpath. Struggling, she stumbled on the rocks as she cradled her precious cargo. She fought against panic as Gabby gasped, coughed, and battled to remain conscious. Jennifer found herself having to pause and regroup her arms around her nana, bracing Gabby's weight against one of her legs before continuing down the pathway. She suddenly began to sing one of her nana's Yiddish melodies to her. As she struggled to keep her balance, Jennifer whispered a mantra of comfort, meant not only for Gabby's benefit but for her own as well.

"You are not alone," she insisted. "You are not alone, do you hear me? You are *not* alone."

27

At Augusta General Hospital, events happened so fast Jennifer felt she'd entered a speed warp. She wasn't even sure how she'd managed to get Gabby back to the car, much less find the hospital. In her rush to seek help she never noticed the blood at the corners of her nana's mouth. Only as the emergency team removed Gabby from the car, placing her swiftly on a stretcher, did Jennifer catch sight of the crimson trail of phlegm on her nana's chin.

They worked on Gabby behind a curtain for what seemed a lifetime to Jennifer. Finally, after successfully stabilizing her, they placed her on an IV drip, fed her oxygen from a mask, and connected her to a host of monitors. It was only then that the attending physician pulled Jennifer aside.

"How long has she been diagnosed with emphysema?"

Jennifer had no idea.

"Her lungs are shot," the doctor informed her. "She appears to have been on medication to control the chronic cough and the wheezing you've no doubt seen."

"Yes," Jennifer said softly. "But she told me it was under control, though I'm sure I should have known better." She lowered her head. "I've been having some personal problems, she was helping me."

"She wasn't really in much of a place to help anybody," the doctor said, shaking his head. "Emphysema's a lung disease that destroys the alveoli, the air sacs. The lungs become less able to expand and contract. People as sick as your grandmother have air sacs that can't really deflate, so they become unable to take in enough air to ventilate. It makes them gasp for breath. Of course being overactive, which I take it she is, does nothing but inflame the situation."

Jennifer's mind reeled with the idea of the physical exertion her nana had put herself through on her behalf. The trip to California to bring her back, the race to find her in the park, this whole extraordinary journey they'd been on.

"She was probably never a candidate for surgery," the doctor concluded. "It might have improved her breathing a bit, but at a certain point it's just an unacceptable risk." The doctor looked at her sadly. "By now, I'm afraid, she's too far gone."

"What does that mean?" Jennifer demanded.

"It means we can keep her on a machine to help her breathe, but she's got a pretty nasty pulmonary infection that's spread to what's left of her lungs. Sometimes there's a genetic disposition to these sorts of things. How did her parents die?"

Jennifer couldn't even begin to share that information. Instead, she just looked at him and said nothing.

"Well," the physician continued. "She'll probably need to be hospitalized unless you can afford home care. At any rate, her suffering won't go on much longer. I'm very sorry. It's truly a miracle she's lasted until now. A real survivor, that one."

Jennifer stared at the doctor, trying to comprehend what he had just said. A few minutes later she stood coatless out in the cold air, in shock. It was happening all over again. Just as it had with her mother. Someone she loved was being torn from her and she was helpless to do anything about it. For a moment it crossed her mind that had she been successful in her attempt at suicide, she wouldn't be going through the heartache she was experiencing right now. But in the next instant she was horrified and ashamed for having had such a thought at all.

And then — and she'd never be able to explain this sensation to another person — Jennifer heard a calming voice from somewhere deep within her. This voice announced that she had it all wrong. This situation wasn't about her or her pain. Nor was it about all that was being lost and the lack of anything to stop it. It was about an opportunity. It was about what Jennifer could do to alleviate her nana's suffering. No, this wasn't a door closing in front of her, shutting her out, but one that was opening, allowing Jennifer into a crucial point in her nana's life — her death.

Jennifer realized that this time, unlike when her mother had died, she wasn't helpless. In fact, she was powerful beyond measure. She could now be there for her nana, giving her love and comfort when she needed it most, just as Gabby had been there for her these past weeks, offering so much of herself, helping Jennifer to embrace life with passion. Maybe that was the gift in all the pain, Jennifer recognized. And she knew she was not about to let this precious moment pass her by. Indeed, she was determined to be part of it.

Later in the room when Gabby opened her eyes, Jennifer was waiting with a smile. "I'm taking you home," she said.

"I was hoping you would say that," Gabby whispered back weakly, somehow managing, even in pain, to flash her trademark grin. A classic Nana move, thought Jennifer, shaking her head in admiration. Making you feel good even if it kills her.

The next day, with Gabby tethered to a portable oxygen tank, Jennifer set out for New York City, her nana stretched out in the backseat. Jennifer said playfully, "Keep your arms, legs, and oxygen masks in the vehicle at all times, ma'am. Sit back and relax. You're in for a smooth ride."

As they took to the road Jennifer glanced into the rearview mirror and caught her nana's eyes. They shone gratefully. Jennifer nodded back, swallowed hard, and eased on the gas.

28

Jennifer contacted Gabby's physician the moment they arrived back in the city. He agreed to come to the apartment to examine his favorite patient. As Jennifer suspected, Dr. Wassner insisted on Gabby's being hospitalized immediately. Gradually, however, he was worn down by an iron-willed Jennifer, whom he found to be every bit as oppositional and assertive as her nana. He had to admit that he did, in fact, concur with the doctor's assessment in Maine. He told Jennifer that he had seen Gabby in the office just before she had flown to California. That trip, he emphasized, was made against his strenuous warning that Gabby was putting herself at risk of infection or worse. Her dramatic response, he vividly recalled, was that there was a family emergency, and that no doctor was going to stop her from going. Certainly her emphysema didn't have a chance. The fact that she was still able to get around and breathe at all at the time was inexplicable, the doctor stated. "She must have willed herself to live these past weeks, that's all I can tell you."

In the end, facing the stubborn opposition of two strong women, he relented. He would respect Gabby's wishes to remain in her home with what time she had left. Replacements for the portable oxygen tank would be delivered along with medication that would help keep her comfortable. As he was leaving, Dr. Wassner turned back to Jennifer. "I was just wondering. Did Gabby at least make it to L.A. in time to help?"

Jennifer paused, looking down. Lifting her face to him, she smiled. "Yes, Doctor," she said with a full heart. "Absolutely."

Jennifer next phoned her father.

"I want you to know that I'm fine. I've never been stronger," she blurted out when her dad answered the phone.

"That's great, Jennifer, but why haven't you —"

"Look, don't start with why I haven't called or anything, all right? Nana's sick. Very sick. She's going to die. And she needs me. So . . . as long as she does, I'm here. Don't send any goons to find me or whatever you had planned . . . Dad."

There was a long silence on the other end of the line. Barry cleared his throat. Jennifer wondered what was going on, prepared for a fight.

"I was just . . ." Barry began, halted, then tried again. "Look, would you like me to fly in. Help out in some way?"

Jennifer was taken aback. She hadn't expected this.

"No, thanks," she replied, surprised but firm nevertheless. "I want this time alone with her, Dad. I need it, all right?"

"Call me, Jennifer," Barry said, his voice subdued and vulnerable in a way Jennifer hadn't remembered. "Let me know if there's anything I can do."

"I will," she promised.

And then her father said something Jennifer never thought she would hear from his lips: "I'm proud of you, and I know your mother would be proud of you as well." There was a pause and then, "Jen, I love you." And he was gone.

After they had hung up, Jennifer stood in the kitchen staring at the phone. Her nana was right, sometimes the gifts come wrapped in pain and other times they hit you smack-dab in the face when you are totally unprepared.

Jennifer sat by Gabby's bedside throughout the day, bringing her meals and tea when she asked for it, running out only to pick up a few groceries at the corner market. She had wanted to have even those things delivered, but Gabby had insisted that she at least get herself a little fresh air. At night Jennifer chose to bed down on the floor in order to be nearer to Gabby in case she needed her in the middle of the night.

They had been home for several days when Jennifer returned from picking up a prescription and found the phone ringing off the hook. To her surprise it was Charlie Sosne, Gabby's stalwart steed from the day Gabby had enlisted him in her search for Jennifer in Central Park. He told her he'd called a few times during the past week or so but never seemed to get them in. It just so happened he would be in the neighborhood that very evening and wondered if he might drop by.

"Nice to hear from you, Charlie," Jennifer said, warming to the sound of his voice. "It's only that . . . it might not be a good idea. My nana's pretty sick right now."

"I'm so sorry," Charlie replied quickly. "I didn't . . . Look, you're right, it's probably not the best time," he added, genuinely concerned.

Jennifer's mind raced. It would be good to see him again. She could use a friend.

"Hey, Charlie." Her voice brightened.

"Maybe it would be all right, you know, for a few minutes. I bet my nana would like that . . . and I would, too."

"Well, great," Charlie responded. "Do you need anything? Groceries, I don't know . . . something?"

"No, but thanks. Around seven?" Jennifer offered.

"Seven, right," Charlie said, adding, "I'll keep it short, I promise."

Jennifer heard the eagerness in his voice and it felt for a moment like oxygen to the heart.

Jennifer hung up only to be hit with second thoughts. Would Gabby really want a visitor in her condition?

"Wonderful, great news," Gabby gleefully responded when Jennifer told her about Charlie. "We could use a little pick-me-up around here."

As the time drew near for Charlie's visit, Gabby had Jennifer prop her up in bed. Catching sight of her pale and drawn face in a hand mirror, she asked for some rouge to dab on her cheeks. "No use scaring the young man," she deadpanned. Jennifer arranged the oxygen mask over Gabby's nose, making sure she could get enough air, and while removing the mirror, caught herself checking out the status of her own looks.

She had to laugh. This wasn't some kind of date, she reminded herself. Her nana was sick and this man they both barely knew was kind enough to want to pay his respects. Who cared what she looked like?

When Charlie arrived that evening he was dressed in solid black with a full-length gray woolen coat. His energy instantly added warmth to the apartment. In one hand he held a single delicate rose, and in the other, a small gift-wrapped silver box. Jennifer smiled at his thoughtfulness and led him in to see her nana. Gabby held out her arms, impressing Jennifer with her effort to let him know how pleased she was to see him. But there was something more going on, Jennifer felt. It was almost as if her nana had expected Charlie to come. But how could she have known that?

Gabby encouraged Charlie to sit down at the edge of the bed so she could see him better.

"I hope I'm not disturbing you," he said apologetically.

"I'm dying, Charlie," Gabby offered, donning her oxygen mask. "How much more *disturbed* can I get?"

An instant uneasiness filled the room at the mention of her impending demise. Jennifer and Charlie exchanged startled glances. But the sounds of ever so soft hoarse laughter instantly erased any tension. You couldn't miss the mischievous twinkle in Gabby's eye, and Jennifer laughed at her nana's lightness. Even now, facing her own death, her nana was managing to teach her about living.

"This is for you," Charlie said, handing the rose to Gabby, who was visibly moved by the gracious gesture.

"It's been a long time since a man gave me a flower, Charlie," Gabby said, an appreciative grin softening her gaunt features. "But I'm an old woman and I'm thinking we don't have the best of prospects together, so maybe you'd do better to give it to my granddaughter, hmm?" she prodded, giving him a not-so-subtle tilt of her head in Jennifer's direction.

"Nana," Jennifer chided her gently, "cut the guy a break."

"No, the flower is for you, Gabby," Charlie insisted. "I have something else for your granddaughter."

He walked over to Jennifer, handing her the small silver box tied with a golden ribbon. Jennifer was unsure what to say, smiling with embarrassment.

"I . . . why would you do this?" she asked, totally nonplussed.

"Stop with all the questions, meydele. A man gives you a present, you open it," Gabby said before ducking back beneath the oxygen mask.

Jennifer slowly removed the gold ribbon and the silver wrapping paper. The box she held in her hands was dark blue and embossed with the emblem of the Central Park Conservancy. Opening it up, she broke into a broad grin. Carefully she pulled out the tiny glass replica of Belvedere Castle, the site where Charlie and her nana had found her that morning. She looked over at Gabby, who nodded her obvious approval beneath the plastic apparatus. Turning back to Charlie, Jennifer smiled, her eyes now searching his.

"What an absolutely lovely thing to do," she said. "I'm not sure why I deserve this, since you and Nana did all the work that day."

The sound coming from the bed was Gabby rather loudly clearing her throat.

"Truth is," Charlie began tentatively, "I'm not really the white knight who rescued the fair maiden that morning a couple of weeks ago. Your grandmother has that distinction. But I figured just maybe the horse might merit some consideration?"

Gabby's eyes opened wide behind her

mask. Jennifer was floored. Yes, she had felt some attraction when he had taken her hand in the park that day, but this? How could a person be so bold about his feelings for her when he didn't really know her? She stared at the gift and her mind seemed to explode with emotion. Everything in her life felt so tenuous. She was just getting back on her feet. She was on the brink of losing her nana. Seeing Charlie standing in front of her now suddenly brought back painful memories of Phillip and that disastrous experience. Was she really ready to jump back into life like this?

"The gift is beautiful, Charlie, and I'm truly flattered. But I'm not really in a place —"

Back on the bed, beneath the oxygen mask, Gabby was beside herself. It was taking enormous restraint for her to hold her tongue. She shouldn't interfere, she told herself. This was her granddaughter's decision to make. *Her* life, *her* gift of a young man's intentions to do with as she thought best. If she wanted to close the door, well, Gabby would just have to let her. On second thought, she figured, maybe the situation was just begging for a little push.

"I don't mean to interrupt," Gabby proclaimed, coughing for good effect.

Jennifer turned to her with a grin and a shake of her head. "What is it, Nana?"

"I just wanted to say, you should pardon the expression, but even a horse gets a cube of sugar every once in a while." And with an impish arch of her brow, Gabby slipped back beneath the mask.

Charlie took a step forward, his boyish but chiseled face reflecting the earnest and unvarnished feelings of a man who knew his own heart. "Listen, Jennifer, I don't know why we met, and I know that my timing is terrible, but I was afraid you might be returning to Los Angeles and I didn't want to miss my chance to tell you . . ." He was searching for the words as impatiently as Jennifer and Gabby were waiting to hear them.

"Look, I never in my life believed that things are, you know what they say, 'meant to be.' I always just figured serendipity was a crock. Sorry about that, Gabby . . . but something about you, Jennifer, that day in the park, I don't know, it stayed with me." He hesitated, considering his words. "I'd just like the opportunity, if you wouldn't mind terribly sometime, to get to know you, and maybe somehow, you might be willing to get to know me. You think that might be possible?"

Jennifer glanced over at Gabby, who appeared, even in her distressed condition, deeply smitten. Looking down at the delicate glass castle, Jennifer knew that something in her had changed. That despite all that was happening, all she had gone through and would yet experience in the days ahead, it was time to accept the gifts being handed her by the universe. More than that, she knew in her heart that she passionately wanted the opportunity to take a first step all over again. She looked up at him, slowly breaking into a smile, nodding at the possibility. "I think I'd like that, Charlie."

Gabby's mask flew off as she shouted "Mazel tov!" and Jennifer had all she could do to calm her down before the coughing began again.

After Jennifer and Charlie exchanged numbers, Charlie bent down and gave Gabby a small kiss on the forehead. Jennifer led Charlie to the door. She cautioned him she would have to go slow, that she didn't know what the future held for her.

"None of us do," Charlie agreed, smiling warmly. "I never thought an old woman would saddle me up and take me for a ride in the park. Life's just full of surprises, I guess."

He made her promise to call if she or Gabby needed anything. And then, with a kiss on her hand, he was gone, leaving Jennifer shaking her head at the way life had of mixing sweetness and sorrow all at once.

The minute she was back in her nana's room, they both dissolved into schoolgirl giggling. It pained Gabby to laugh this much, but it felt good all the same. The joy in the room, however, was short-lived, as Gabby grew weak from the excitement. They both discovered she had coughed up some blood into the mask, which Jennifer removed as they exchanged silent glances. After she had replaced the mask with a sterile one, Jennifer sadly apologized for causing Gabby to overexert herself by allowing Charlie to visit that evening. But Gabby quieted her, bringing a finger to her lips and whispering, "Sheyna meydele, I wouldn't have missed it for the world."

Later, after her nana had fitfully fallen asleep, Jennifer took out the journal Gabby had given her in Maine and began to write furiously. Late into the night she sat there on the floor of her nana's bedroom, pouring out everything inside of her, all that she was now able to feel, onto the page.

29

For ten days they did their best to live a lifetime of sharing. But Gabby's condition had rapidly declined, just as the doctors had predicted. Even worse than having her once spirited voice be reduced to a hoarse whisper was Gabby's inability to muster even a shred of her trademark energy, the struggle for breath sapping any strength she might still possess. Gabby was now unable to get out of the bed to go to the bathroom, requiring Jennifer to take care of her personal needs, something she accomplished with a quiet dignity, helping to minimize Gabby's initial distress and obvious embarrassment.

At the same time, Gabby's physician had arranged for a nurse to come in to assess the situation. The middle-aged woman hailing from Great Britain was ruddy of face and steely of disposition. She was eager, professional, and dedicated to doing the right thing by her patients. She wasted no time recommending yet again that Gabby be removed to the hospital, insisting it was the least that must be done now that she had lost her mobility. She argued that while she respected terminal patients' desire to remain at home, Gabby's rapid deterioration required highly trained care. Jennifer noted that the nurse spoke in the clipped, dispassionate manner the British do so well, insisting that only a proper hospital staff would be in a position to administer by IV and monitor the drugs to manage Gabby's pain.

But after a few moments of listening to the take-charge nurse's laundry list of why she should be immediately transferred to a medical facility, Gabby cut her off with a wagging finger of disapproval. Gathering herself up as best she could, she addressed the woman with measured defiance:

"Pain is part of life, Nurse. And from one who knows, let me tell you a little secret — it is not the worst part. Being alone, without loved ones, without family — now that is far worse. I want to be in my own bed. So? It's familiar. And as you can see" — she gestured toward Jennifer, managing to produce for her a little wink — "here I am blessed with the crème de la crème of nurses."

Exasperated, yet convinced she had met up with an immovable object, the nurse let out a deep breath, like a balloon deflating.

She was, as Gabby would comment later, a trouper, and turned her attention to the task of showing Jennifer how best to alleviate some of Gabby's discomfort through steadily increasing the dosage of a new pain medication she had brought, as well as by regulating the oxygen levels to keep up with her nana's steadily decreasing ability to draw breath. As Jennifer accompanied her to the door, the fastidious woman informed her that when the time came, Jennifer should call her nana's doctor. He would take care of the arrangements Gabby had made some time ago. The nurse wished her luck and turned to leave; she caught Jennifer thoroughly off-guard by suddenly turning back and giving her a comforting hug.

That night, as was now customary, Jennifer opened her journal to record the day's gifts with Gabby. But this night was going to be different. Gabby clearly had something else in mind, motioning Jennifer closer so she could look into her eyes. Jennifer crossed to the bed, kneeling down beside her with a curious smile.

"What is it, Nana?"

With great effort, Gabby spoke her heart. "I have something for you, Jennifer. I want to give it to you before I run out of time."

"Nana, you've given me enough," Jennifer protested softly.

"In the top of my dresser you'll find an envelope."

Jennifer dutifully crossed to the dresser, opened the top drawer, and reached in through a tangle of stockings and assorted socks.

"In the back somewhere. It's there, keep looking," Gabby prodded weakly.

Jennifer felt her hand close around the envelope, and she drew it forth from the drawer.

"Yes," Gabby nodded. "Please, bring it over here."

Jennifer complied, placing the small white slightly crumpled item in her nana's hands and kneeling down beside her.

Jennifer watched Gabby run her fingers slowly over the surface of the envelope, as if it held the greatest of treasures. Gabby looked into the quizzical eyes of her granddaughter and smiled warmly.

"Something I didn't share with you. Back when I was in that attic in Poland, I asked Mrs. Pulaski if I might have a pencil and a few pieces of paper so I could keep a record of every day's gifts."

"You kept a journal there?" Jennifer asked, awed and surprised.

Even in her frail state, Gabby seemed amused. "Yes, if you could call some stray papers a journal." She smiled. "I wrote on every spare surface of the papers, writing there what I saw, what I heard, or the beautiful things I remembered, anything that gave me even a slight relief from the misery of my circumstances." She coughed, turned away a moment to compose herself, then drew back to face Jennifer, whose eyes never left her.

"I had been writing on the last of these precious few pieces of paper when Mrs. Pulaski burst in to warn me of her neighbor's suspicions. There was no time to do anything but run. I stuffed that last page into my clothing."

Jennifer's heart beat faster as Gabby pulled from the envelope a wrinkled, ragged piece of paper crammed full of tiny writing.

"This is the final page, Jennifer. I wanted you to have it."

Jennifer's eyes filled with tears as she stared down at the precious paper in her hands. It was yellow from age and the foreign writing upon it had faded, but the letters were still decipherable. The penciled markings seemed to veer off in all directions, in circles, packed into the corners.

She turned it over to find Gabby had used every square inch of space on both sides. Jennifer looked at her nana, her quivering lips unable to find the words.

"You look after that now for me, all right?" Gabby said, reaching for Jennifer's hand and kissing the back of it tenderly.

Jennifer nodded through her tears.

"Come. Look how old this paper is. Soon no one will be able to make out these words. I'm going to translate the Polish for you so you can place them in your journal. That way" — she paused — "they will not die."

Gabby's voice was hoarse and she gave her granddaughter a brave smile. Jennifer reached for her, enfolding Gabby in her arms, and softly wept. After several minutes, Gabby helped her to wipe away her tears. Then, pulling herself upright, Jennifer took up her journal and recorded all that her nana read to her, Gabby's final gifts.

She wrote down *memories* Gabby had once recorded: the smell of the kitchen when her mother had been baking, the way her father's eyes had danced when he laughed, the look of excitement in Anna's eyes when she laced on her skates. Jennifer took down the *sounds* her nana had once savored, imprisoned in her attic: the soft drumming of the falling rain; the morning song of the local bird she never was able to glimpse; her own heart beating within her, a reminder she was still alive. And, as her nana fought to make out her own writing and then render the words into English, Jennifer received from her lips *images* that had encouraged Gabby's once caged spirit: the hopeful smile on Mrs. Pulaski's face each evening; a snowman Gabby had viewed from the attic window, letting her know there were children still at play; her reflection in a broken mirror; the way she saw her family's faces in her own.

When Jennifer had finished writing down every one of the gifts her nana was able to decipher, she read them back. Gabby nodded. Then, turning to her granddaughter, she spoke in as clear a voice as she could muster. "I want you to know something, meydele. And believe this with all of your heart. This precious time we have shared together has crowned my life with hope." Gabby had trouble swallowing but reached out her hand and cradled Jennifer's gently within it. "I want you to always know that you, sweet girl, are *enough*. And that you will always deserve . . . more *life!*"

Tears brimmed in both their eyes. With great effort, Gabby took the pen and journal from her granddaughter's hand. Jennifer watched as Gabby slowly scrawled a message:

To my greatest gift, my granddaughter —
Listen for me in your heart,
that is where I choose now to live . . .
for that is my heaven.
Love, Nana

30

Gabby died the next morning.

A bountiful crisp dawn had just begun showing its bright face to the city when she drew her final breath, turning her head toward the light pouring through the bedroom window. She left cradled in the grateful arms of a granddaughter to whom she had given the gift of life as surely as Lili had in giving birth to Jennifer.

Few people gathered at the graveside out on Long Island. Other than Dr. Wassner, Gabby's physician, and of course, Frieda Steinberg, Jennifer hadn't really known whom to call. She had left a message for her dad telling him of Gabby's passing. And she had called Charlie. It surprised her at how grateful she was when he arrived. He walked over to her just prior to the graveside service, giving Jennifer a comforting and much-needed hug before taking his place a few feet away with the handful of mourners. As the coffin was lowered and the mourner's kaddish was recited, Jennifer's tears fell freely and gratefully upon the earth, tempered with a measure of peaceful satisfaction. For her nana now lay buried next to her beloved, Itzik.

Earlier, as the only family member, she was invited to view her nana's body before burial. She had reached out to brush a few wisps of white hair back into place and then slipped a photo of Gabby, Itzik, and Lili on vacation in Maine she'd found in her nana's drawer into the simple wooden coffin. She chose to keep for herself another photograph she'd come across, this one of Gabby as a young adult ice-skating, her face filled with a glorious radiance.

As she left the cemetery, something soft and wet landed on Jennifer's nose. Looking up through her tears, she grinned. It was snowing. Charlie accompanied her back to the apartment, where a few of her nana's friends, unable to make it out to the island, gathered for the customary shivah prayers and meal of consolation. From his perch on the window seat Charlie followed Jennifer as she helped lay out the food Frieda had prepared. There was enough there to feed a small army, which didn't surprise Jennifer at all. She did her best to make small talk with individuals she barely knew. Finally, after helping the last of Gabby's friends to a plate of hand-sliced turkey, potato salad, and coleslaw, Jennifer turned away, searching for a respite. Her gaze connected with Charlie's. He waved and acknowledged what she was feeling with a shake of his head and a smile. She nodded back, pleased that there was someone her age in the room and that he seemed to understand how strange this all was for her. She started toward him and Charlie rose to meet her, but before they reached each other Frieda thrust a phone toward Jennifer, one hand over the receiver. Jennifer hadn't even heard it ring.

"Your father," whispered Frieda, eyebrows raised in a way that reminded Jennifer of her nana's impish silent commentary when a look said more than words. Charlie nodded and backed away as Jennifer retreated to the hallway to take the call.

"Hi," Jennifer said into the receiver.

"How are you doing, Jen?" Barry asked with concern.

"I'm okay. Funeral was nice. She would have liked it," Jennifer responded in a low-key voice. There was a sudden swell of voices spilling out of the living room, sending her farther down the hallway.

"Jen, I know this has been a hard time. Your nana was lucky to have you with her through all of it," Barry offered.

Jennifer's eyes fell upon the photos on the wall. She stared at her mother feeding a horse as a young child and then at Gabby, who seemed to be looking back at her with a smile dipped in light.

"I was the lucky one," Jennifer whispered.

"Jen . . ." he started before his voice broke off. She heard her father clearing his throat, struggling with emotion. She waited.

"Do you have plans now?" he asked, though it seemed to Jennifer there was something else on his mind.

"I haven't even thought about it," Jennifer suddenly realized. "I'll come back for a bit, I guess, then see from there."

"Good," Barry said softly.

There was an uncomfortable silence and then Barry spoke up. "Look, Jen, I was hoping, I know you probably won't want to do this, but . . . day after tomorrow is Thanksgiving. I know you haven't forgiven me for a lot of things. Do you think there's any chance you might head back here and have dinner with . . . your family?"

Jennifer closed her eyes tight at the sound of that word. A host of emotions were running through her. With so much going on inside, she knew she would have to take it at her own pace. He was trying, she had to give him that. She still didn't know about forgiving him. That would be hard. But maybe a meal. She could do that.

"Okay, Dad," she heard herself say quietly. "Yes, I think I'd like that. I'll be there."

Barry seemed genuinely overcome, and then, pulling himself together, he effused, "That's great, Jennifer, your little sister, Briana, she'll love getting to know you."

He was off spinning a story of how great everything was going to be and how they would do things together and would she like to join them on a trip to Aspen and . . . but Jennifer's attention was elsewhere. She was thinking of that little baby, the Chihuahua. She'd never really acknowledged that she had a little sister. Never taken the time to meet her. Maybe, as Gabby would say, this was a gift it was time to receive. A m'chayah she would have called it, the little things that could put life back into you. She tuned back in to her father, who was still going on.

"I'll see you day after tomorrow, Dad," Jennifer interrupted, putting the brakes on her father's effusive verbal roll. "Okay?"

Uncharacteristically Barry stopped speaking. There was a beat. He took a breath. "Thank you," he said softly, adding quickly, "and Jennifer?"

"Yes?"

"You and your nana — you were both lucky to have each other. I get that now. Bye."

And he was gone. Jennifer let that thought wash over her. She stared once more at Gabby's photo on the wall. Then, turning back, she found Charlie waiting for her in the doorway.

"Hey," she said in surprise.

"Everything all right with your dad?" he asked, concern furrowing his brow.

"I'm not sure I'd go that far," she quipped lightly, "but, yeah, I told him I'd join him for Thanksgiving. We'll see how that goes."

"Good. Good for you." Charlie smiled, nodding his head. He suddenly looked worried. "Does that mean you'll be leaving New York for good?"

Jennifer suddenly felt an overwhelming desire to be anywhere but in a house of mourning.

"Let's get some air," she said. Hurriedly donning coats, the two of them slipped out of the apartment without a word.

Outside on the stoop they stood silently looking up at the now clear sky. So many feelings were flowing through Jennifer. The reality of having buried Gabby that day, the prospects of returning to L.A. for the first time since everything had happened, Thanksgiving dinner with her father and his family, and yes, there was Charlie. She pulled her coat up around her ears more snugly. The brisk cold felt good on her face, but after a few moments she began to shiver. There was so much she was facing now. Gabby was gone and she would have to do it alone.

Charlie instinctively drew near, putting an arm around her and pulling her close for warmth.

"Jennifer," he began, turning toward her, "I've never known anyone who loved her grandmother more and backed it up by the way she cared for her."

Jennifer nodded, whispering "Thank you," but his words unleashed the tears and she began to cry softly. He held her, speaking what was in his heart.

"I don't know how long you plan to be in L.A., but if it would be all right with you, I'd love to come out there and have you show me around."

Jennifer pulled back and looked up at him. She could see the hope there. Charlie reached out to wipe the tears from her eyes and grinned expectantly.

"How could I say no to a man who gave my nana her last rose," she replied with a grin. She figured she might have to slow

Charlie down, if only because he was galloping so damn fast. She'd been hurt that way. Still, she had to admit it would be pretty nice being pursued, and across the country no less! Who knows, maybe she'd even end up living in New York. Jennifer had the distinct feeling that Gabby was getting one hell of a kick out of this somewhere, insisting she get credit for having been the matchmaker.

And then, suddenly remembering something, Jennifer asked a slightly perplexed Charlie to make her apologies to Frieda and the others. She had something she needed to do, she said. With a promise to be back soon, Jennifer headed off alone into the night.

Jennifer walked with determination, playing and replaying memories of the past several weeks and the journey she'd made with her nana. In short time she had traversed the pathway in Central Park, arriving at her destination — Wollman Rink.

Looking out at the white iridescent oval, Jennifer smiled with curiosity. Taking in the lights and the crowd, hearing the music, she couldn't help but think of Gabby and her sister, Anna, skating across an icy pond in the little Polish town of their childhood. And even though she had never ice-skated before, now seemed as good a time as any to try. Which is how she found herself, a bit wobbly at first, but with the increasing assurance of one who'd done time on Rollerblades, skating her heart out. The edges of Jennifer's skates kicked ice chips into the air. They landed on her face, cold and alive. She took in the November moon shining overhead, the night sky dancing with shimmering stars.

Jennifer moved now with a freedom and wondrous abandon. She skated for Anna, whom Gabby wished all her life to see on the ice again. She skated for her mother, Lili, whose spirit she knew for certain was there with her now. She skated for herself, embracing the electric passion of being alive. Most of all, she skated for her nana, who had altered the course of her life.

Jennifer moved with an energy that startled her, acquiring speed as she circled the rink to the rhythm of the music. At first she glided timidly in procession with others. Before long, however, as she gained her legs and confidence, Jennifer discovered she had left the crowd behind, turning now to her own inner music, pouring into her movements tears and laughter and the memory of the extraordinary woman who had rescued her.

She skated into the night until her legs gave out. And then, sprawling out in snow near the rink, Jennifer lay there, looking up at the sparkling night sky. Like the pages she had yet to fill in her journal and like the white surface of the ice beneath her, Jennifer could see that her future, as her nana had said, was intriguingly blank and full of possibilities. It was waiting for her to write it, to fill the pages of her tomorrows with the life she alone could create.

Perspiring and out of breath, Jennifer was suddenly acutely aware of her own heart beating within her. It was as if she were listening to this powerful rhythm for the first time.

Placing a hand on her chest, Jennifer closed her eyes and whispered with gratitude: "I hear you, Nana. Oh, yes, I hear you."

About the Author

Jan Goldstein is an award-winning poet and playwright and the author of two works of nonfiction. He lives with his wife, Bonnie, and their family in Los Angeles. Find out more about Jan and *All That Matters* at www.jangoldstein.com.

The employees of Thorndike Press hope you have enjoyed this Large Print book. All our Thorndike and Wheeler Large Print titles are designed for easy reading, and all our books are made to last. Other Thorndike Press Large Print books are available at your library, through selected bookstores, or directly from us.

For information about titles, please call:

(800) 223-1244

or visit our Web site at:

www.gale.com/thorndike
www.gale.com/wheeler

To share your comments, please write:

Publisher
Thorndike Press
295 Kennedy Memorial Drive
Waterville, ME 04901